Cajun Zombie Chronicles:
Book Two

THE
ISLAND DEAD

by

S. L. Smith

HOLY WATER BOOKS

Cajun Zombie Chronicles: Book Two
The Island Dead

ISBN-13: 978-1-950782-29-1 (Holy Water Books)

HOLY WATER BOOKS
At the unexpected horizons of the New Evangelization

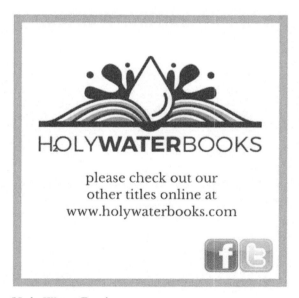

HOLYWATERBOOKS

please check out our
other titles online at
www.holywaterbooks.com

Cover design by Holy Water Books

Cajun Zombie Chronicles: Book Two
THE ISLAND DEAD

Table of Contents

PROLOGUE:

BROOKS PLANTATION

The five vehicles bumped along a dirt road. The road led back behind a line of large white homes that overlooked the glittering sweep of False River. The land beyond and behind the homes was filled with pastures and orchards. Beyond this, there lay a mile or more of thick woodland. It was creased here and there by shooting lanes for deer-hunting, but, other than this, it had been untouched for over a hundred years.

The shadows of the trees fell across the line of vehicles as they followed the dirt road about a thousand yards into the forest. There, the dirt road formed a circle driveway around the old Moore plantation. The road grew quite a bit bumpier as the roots of ancient live oak trees emerged from the hard-packed soil. The caravan of trucks slowed to a stop. They had spaced themselves around the house so that they surrounded it on four sides, leaving the lead vehicle, Old Blue, pointing back out the direction they had come.

Isherwood slid out the front seat of the Jeep that he had chosen from the dealership. It, along with two of the other vehicles, had been heavily modified for the world's changed circumstances. Spare tires were mounted along the sides and back of the Jeep to provide for quick pit stops as well as a buffer between the car and oncoming swarms of the undead. Turrets had been cut in the rooftops of the Jeep, as well as Old Blue and an Escalade. Gun racks had been mounted on the insides of the vehicles, grill guards installed, chain link fencing installed along the windows, and they'd all been sprayed down with black paint. They had left the other two vehicles as-is. These were an armored troop transport and a Humvee that had been liberated from the local National Guard armory.

Isherwood thumbed his radio on. "St. Mary's, this is Isherwood. Whoever's listening – I think we've found ourselves a new bug-out location. We've just arrived at the home of Brooks Moore. Over."

"Roger that." A voice came back. It was Vanessa, a black woman that they'd found near death in what remained of the National Guard Armory. Miraculously, they had also found her boy, Le'Marcus, among very few other survivors. "I'll tell Sara and the others. Over and out." *Click-shhh.*

Sara was Isherwood's wife. She was the one who had directed the men to the Moore plantation to search as a possible weapons cache. The men were on their way to rescue Sara's family, which were trapped at their camp in Whiskey Bay, surrounded by a massive swarm of thousands of zombies.

The other men were getting out of their vehicles, too. There was Justin getting out of the Escalade with his trusty ArmaLite rifles. Justin and his family, as well as Patrick, who was driving Old Blue, and his family had been found by Isherwood about a week ago, as Isherwood was leading a long line of zombies out of the town like the Pied Piper of St. Maryville. They had been friends for years and were each extremely lucky to have survived, let alone together and with their families. This group of three men and their families had formed the nucleus of a small but growing community of survivors sheltering behind the high fences of St. Mary's Church. The community was led by Monsignor Bellarmine, an older priest who had provided an indomitable spirit to the community as well as vision for its future.

They had been joined only days ago by Father Simeon and Marshall, who were getting out of the Humvee and troop transport, respectively. Father Simeon, who was called "Padre" by most everyone, had been the young pastor of a church in Morganza, not far from St. Maryville. The others were slowly discovering that the priest, who always wore a black cassock, seemed to be strangely well-suited for the Apocalypse.

Vanessa had achieved radio contact with Glenn LaGrange, Sara's father trapped with his family at Whiskey Bay, within a day's span of the men fighting off back-to-back calamities. The first had been the two or three thousand zombies belched out of the Mississippi River and advancing on St. Anne's Church in Morganza. The second had been rescuing Isherwood's daughter, Emma Claire, after she had been kidnapped by a radical group of survivors who had become, they later found out, something of a doomsday cult. The men and the community had weathered both of these calamities seemingly unscathed. However, their supplies of ammunition had been radically depleted just in time to hear Glenn's calls for help.

Now, as they traveled to Whiskey Bay, they were being slowed by the need to replenish their stores of ammo. There was just no telling how many zombies would need to be killed near Whiskey Bay, as it lay directly adjacent to the raised roadway of Interstate 10. They had developed a low-tech strategy to fight the zombies designed to use their own numbers and corpses against them. They would establish a kill zone at a specified radius, typically seventy-five yards from where they circled the wagons. There was still good skull penetration, they had found, at this range for their .22 rifles. Of course, after successfully employing this strategy several times, they were now mostly out of .22-caliber bullets. They would drop the zombies at seventy-five yards, where they would begin to mound up. Eventually, once the mound became difficult to climb, the zombies would start spilling around the edges. The piles of corpses would grow and grow until they formed a circular barricade all around their position. Once this happened, they'd just shoot the zombies' heads as they crested the mounds.

The raids they had already undertaken along the way had been oddly fruitful. Though they had raided the National Guard armory early on, they had yet to visit the police and sheriff's stations. The police station, though otherwise destroyed in what appeared to be the officers' last stand, was a veritable honey pot of 9mm ammunition. All of the police station's firearms, whether pistol or rifle, had been made for 9mm, as well. They thanked God for the chief's foresight, or whoever had made the decision to stick with the 9mm. Isherwood was especially grateful, as the score perfectly matched his own stockpile of pistol ammo. There were enough 9mm rifles found at the police station, in addition to what they already had – Justin's AR-15 were sized for 9mm, as well – to fully re-equip each man of their group with two rifles. They had to alternate rifles due to over-heated during sustained use.

Unlike the police station, the sheriff's office had already been picked clean. This worried Isherwood, but there *were* signs that the sheriff's armory had been raided early on during the apocalypse. This was now the third residence they had raided en route to Whiskey Bay. The raids had been fruitful. These had been the homes of known hunters, but the rescue party had been slowed there by the burials.

"Who lives here, again?" Patrick asked. "The Vampire Lestat?"

Father Simeon called over to them in a hushed tone. He was rounding one corner of the large house and had stopped outside the carport. "Did y'all see these?" He asked, pointing with a Glock 19 to a row of two nearly brand new and matching Land Rovers and a much older work truck. He pressed a finger along the back window of the first Land Rover, and showed it to the others.

"What is it, Padre?" Marshall asked approaching from around the other side of the house.

"I'd say about two weeks of dust," the priest answered. "Watch out. Possible suicides."

Isherwood had started climbing up the wide steps that led up to the back porch. A deep porch wrapped around the entire house and was raised a whole story above ground level. Isherwood's booted feet made hollow, booming thuds on the steps as he ascended them. "Guess that works as well as knocking on the door," Justin remarked on the heavy footfalls.

Isherwood put one boot on the porch and waited. He stood still, listening for the clumsy sounds of undead within. There was some kind of movement, he decided. It wasn't moving, though, so it must be isolated or confined.

9

Isherwood had both feet on the gray boards of the porch now. The others were starting to follow him up the stairs behind him. The back door was broad and heavy. The top half of it was beveled glass, but easy enough to see through. He angled his head to stare into the crack between the door and the jam. *Hmmph.* He mumbled quizzically and reached for the oval brass door knob. It was unlocked! He turned back in surprise to the others. He turned the knob and, though it was a heavy oak door, it swung open smoothly and lightly.

The door opened into a broad hallway that ran the full length of the house to the front door, which was a twin to the back door. A heavy fog of dust reflected in the light that shined through the two doors. Isherwood placed one tentative foot onto the dark, wide-planked floor boards of the hallway. There was only a soft thud, so he brought his other foot forward. This one creaked loudly, a deafening noise through the cavernous home.

Instead of more heavy footfalls coming in behind him, Isherwood's heart leapt as the pitter-pat of little feet erupted from the other end of the hallway. It was a little girl, barefoot, and in her night clothes. She was moving fast, just fast enough for Isherwood to question whether she was living or dead. The light of the front doorway cast her face in shadow. He didn't know what was coming for him. He started backing up, retreating to the half-light of the porch.

"What'cha got there?" Justin asked from the porch.

"Not sure. Can't see. Guns at the ready – she's coming too fast."

They waited outside the door in a semi-circle. Their pistols were drawn and pointing low into the darkness of the open door. They waited. The sound of the bare feet grew softer and was gone.

"Nah-uh," Patrick grunted. "What was that?"

"It was a little girl. Y'all didn't see her?" Isherwood was shaking his head. "I would've bet she was one of them."

"I don't know." Marshall said. "They don't usually stop coming, y'know?"

"Shoot, man." Patrick said with a look of revulsion. "I don't want to go in some old Anne Rice house with little half-zombie girls running around, just waiting to jump out from old settees and rip out my Achilles'. It's like Pet Sematary or something."

Justin rolled his eyes. "Well, thanks for putting *that* in my head."

"Think she could be feral?" Padre asked.

"Feral?" Justin asked. "S'that some kind of new zombie?"

"Nah," Isherwood shook his head. He hadn't taken his eyes on the doorway. "It's like *Nell*, you know that weird movie with Jodie Foster. A wild child. I don't, Padre. Could just be some kind of psychotic break. What the heck happened here?"

"Only one way to find out." Justin said leading the others through the door.

"Right," Isherwood said, following him into the hallway. "We need to get on to Whiskey Bay."

"We could just skip this place," Marshall suggested. He was still standing on the porch, watching the line of trees that encircled the house.

"If Sara's right," Isherwood said, turning into the house's back parlor. "What we find here might be the difference between success and zombie food around I-10."

They were all soon inside the house. They had searched the first floor and found very little. There was a well-stocked kitchen and a refrigerator that was still cool on the inside. The rest of the floor was decorated with antiques, heirloom furniture, and window dressings, but nothing useful for wholesale zombie slaughter.

Isherwood was back in the hallway and looking through the front door. Justin was standing near him, facing down the hallway. "No sign of that little girl, Isherwood. You sure that Jeep wasn't pushing some monoxide through the vents? Some 'shrooms, maybe? But, seriously, what if you saw a ghost – I mean, I'm open to believing a lot of new things since the dead starting walking."

"Dude," Isherwood said shaking his head absentmindedly. "I don't know what's going on around here."

Heavy footfalls began converging on the hallway. Padre and Marshall entered the hallway from opposite sides. Marshall was shaking his head, indicating that the place was a bust. They just stood there looking at each other awkwardly for a moment until Padre wrinkled his brow, and asked, "Where's Patrick?" His absence had apparently escaped everyone else's notice.

"That's a *very* good question." Isherwood said tilting his head to listen.

"Wow, anyone else's head feel funny?" Justin asked. "I'm not sure I would've even noticed he was missing, if you hadn't said anything."

Marshall had turned to look behind him. "He was just in the dining room with me. It was just a second ago." The other men followed Marshall into room. The table was set. Twelve place settings were symmetrically spaced around the long table. It must have been the family's finest porcelain and crystal, or else the family was wealthy enough to have jettisoned the idea of casual dining. "He's just *gone*." Marshall said looking around the room.

"Who's gone?" A new voice asked suddenly. It was Patrick walking out of the shadowy corner of the dining room where two long ornate cupboards appeared to converge.

"You, actually." Padre said matter-of-factly.

"My bad! Sorry, guys." Patrick said excitedly. "I think I found something. That corner is sort of an optical illusion – the walls don't exactly meet right and there's a passage that –" He stopped speaking suddenly. If there had been more light, they might have seen the color drain from his cheeks.

They all looked around to see what Patrick was seeing. They realized with a jolt that there was more than just the five men standing around the table. There was a shadow standing at the head of the table. Her small silhouette was illuminated by the dim light passing through the white gauze draped across the windows.

11

The men were frozen by the shock of the moment. They started backing away almost unconsciously. They were moving towards Patrick and his corner. The girl must have sensed their fear and apprehension, and she lunged for the one nearest her. Isherwood and most of the others blinked at the violence of the child's movements. They heard, rather than saw, what came next. There was a sharp smack and the girl was suddenly lost from view. Padre had been the one closest to her. He had moved quickly and decisively, knocking the girl's head with the butt of his pistol.

"Cold, Padre. Stone cold." Justin was nodding in appreciation. "Glad you did that, 'cause I was about to scream like a little girl."

"At least she's not a ghost," Isherwood added. "Zombies and humans are all I can handle right now."

Marshall rummaged something out of his pocket. "Here, use these." They were two black plastic zip ties. "You know, for her feet and hands."

"Dude," Patrick complained. "It's just a little girl."

Justin rounded on his friend. "Little girl? Did you not just see that? That little thing had fangs!"

Padre quietly took the zip ties and secured the girl, also placing her in a chair so she would be comfortable. "Patrick? Tell me you've found the bat cave."

Patrick shook his head as if lost in fog. "Right, yeah. This way."

They followed Patrick into and through the corner of the room. The walls seemed to meet at the corner but didn't, somehow. They passed around a wall into what first appeared to be a dark pit, but which they soon discovered, as the floor fell away beneath them, was a stairway.

"Why did you even go down into all these freaky darkness, Patrick, with that little girl still running around?" Justin asked. "Pet Sematary, hello?"

"Tell you the truth, I sorta fell into this thing, and—!" He said with a flourish. "There's this." As he said it, they abruptly became aware of the line of light at the bottom of a doorway at the foot of the stairs. The line grew suddenly larger, blinding them. As their eyes adjusted, they realized the room beyond was lit and with *electric* lights.

"No friggin' way," Justin mumbled as his jaw slackened in awe and surprise. Marshall whistled as he clamped his hands around another stair railing as they overlooked the two-story expanse.

Isherwood was nodding, dazed as before. "This oughta put us over the top for Whiskey Bay."

As they looked around, they tried to believe what they were seeing. All the various armories they had raided, including the trip to Wal-Mart, was maybe half of what they were now seeing. It was an enormous man cave. Despite being in southern Louisiana where the water table was basically at ground level, the basement they had entered included a sub-basement. They were surrounded by something of a museum. The walls were studded with examples of the best hunting rifles the world had to offer. Most all of the assembled weapons were modern, but they were several antique military pieces, as well. One wall was dedicated to hand-to-hand combat weapons.

"Mother of God!" Isherwood squealed. He was actually clapping his hands in giddiness like a school boy. "This is the only thing I'd trade my Louisville Slugger for," he said, looking at a tall rack of swords. It was an international collection spanning several centuries of development. There was a short Roman sword, a gladius; a Scottish claymore, like the one Braveheart used in the movie; a Shaolin spade; a Roman pilum, a javelin-like spear; and an assortment of Samurai katanas.

Isherwood was staring up at the three katanas. They were each labelled. The lowest one read "Heisei" and looked almost new. The label also read "Howard Clark". The other two looked much older and we're labelled "Taisho (WWI)" and "Showa (WWII)".

In the midst of his mirth and merriment, Justin sidled up to Isherwood. "You'll shoot your eye out, kid," he said, briefly shaking Isherwood out of his trance. "You, uh, know how to use any of this stuff?"

"Those are legit katanas, man." Isherwood said, pointing. "I'm pretty sure that claymore's over five hundred years old, too."

"Cool, but can you use any of it? I know you're pretty good with a bat, but this isn't exactly a good time to start practicing, you know?"

"I don't know. I took some Aikido, went to an afternoon demonstration of Kempo. I know the basic motions. Thing is, Justin, these things might be virtually indestructible. Bats break. Guns are just clubs without bullets. But," he said taking the Howard Clark down from the rack. "This could get me through a lot, a lot of zombies."

"Okay, yeah. Sure, so could a lightsaber." Justin agreed. "But you actually drop one of those things and you're out a leg or a kid, knowhaddamean?"

Isherwood nodded at his friend and conceded that he was right. As he did so, he strapped the katana sword and scabbard across his back and placed his nicked and blood-stained Louisville Slugger in its place on the wall.

"Hey, come check this out," a voice suddenly boomed through the metal room. It was Father Simeon. He was looking down into a little sitting area, where a Chesterfield leather couch and two matching chairs were centered on a low coffee table. There was a thick drinking glass sitting on the table. A stain marred the wooden table beneath the glass, as though water had been allowed to sit there too long though it had long-since evaporated.

"You mean, none of us noticed the smell of rot?" Patrick asked incredulously. "We're getting too soft." They were all staring down at a withered corpse of a balding man. He was no zombie. He had clearly died of a self-inflicted gunshot wound to his head.

"A *suicide?*" Justin roared. "Are you kidding me? This guy had everything, *everything* he needed to survive in the apocalypse and probably for as long as he wanted. All his doors were unlocked, too — no sign of zombies ever even coming out here. Didn't even have to lift a finger to defend himself. What a waste."

Father Simeon spoke up in explanation, as he rarely did. "He had everything. Everything, but the will to live. No wonder that little girl upstairs went nuts. She was all alone in the house with the corpse of her father."

Isherwood was shaking his head. "But there were two."

"Two?" Marshall asked. "Two what?"

"Two Land Rovers." Isherwood answered. "That couldn't have been an extra, just for the heck of it. That little girl wasn't driving anything. I'm thinking there's still more in the house, probably was married."

"Yeah? So," Justin dismissed the idea. "We'll probably just find her in similar condition beside a long-gone glass *or bottle* of whiskey. She's probably upstairs all dried out in a claw-footed bathtub."

"I'm just saying," Isherwood put up a hand. "That little girl's likely been running around with the corpses of *both* parents just staring back at her. No wonder she's gone 'round the bend. What d'we do with her?"

"All we can," Padre answered simply. "And for as long as we can. She might even surprise us."

Justin kicked the corpse's leather seat. "Thanks, buddy. You just check out, and we're left picking up the pieces."

"Yeah," Isherwood smiled. "But they're some *really* nice pieces, right? These supplies will get us through Whiskey Bay, most likely, *and* keep us afloat for a long, long time. Just those katanas are a treasure. Besides, the girl might just come out of it."

"Sure," Patrick smiled uncertainly. "And pour strychnine down the well."

"It's cool." Marshall shrugged. "She can ride in the troop transport. We can lock her in and she can howl as much as she wants. No one gonna hear her over that diesel engine."

Isherwood nodded. "You heard the man. Let's start loading up. If we can find another 10,000 rounds for the .22LRs and the 9mms, I think we'll be good. We can round that out with specialty ammo if you take a liking to something, but let's try to stick to guns of same or similar calibers." At his instructions, the other four men started spreading back out again. Justin had already found a little cart for wheeling loads to the stairways. "Oh hey, did anyone see any manufacturing stuff?"

Brooks had apparently preferred the .44 caliber firearms to the 9mm, like Isherwood. One entire wall was dedicated to the caliber. There were about twenty magnum pistols, some long barrel antique and modern Colts, as well as two pairs of the Smith & Wesson Model 29 along with an array of holsters. "Dude, must've been a Dirty Harry fan, eh?" Justin remarked.

"You feel lucky?" Patrick laughed. "Well, do ya, *punk*?"

Along with the revolvers, there were about fifteen .44 magnum caliber lever-action rifles. There was a pair of Henry Big Boys, which looked to be straight out of the Wild West, with their shiny brass receivers and octagonal barrels. Padre asked if anybody minded if he claimed these.

"No problem, Padre." Patrick winked. "They go well with that cassock. Sort of a *Two Mules for Sister Sara* look."

Isherwood passed back by the .44 caliber wall a few minutes later pushing a load of 9mm ammo boxes. "Good God." He stammered. Father Simeon had found a double back harness for the Henry rifles and a double holster and gun and ammo belt for the revolvers. "That's just about the most beautiful thing I've ever seen." Isherwood said, inspecting the harness and how the rifles were held inside the leather sheaths. "Man, that's awesome. And don't let anybody tell you brown leather doesn't go with black. We'll just let those kinds of rules collapse with civilization."

"Agreed," Padre nodded. "And I'm bringing back beer with breakfast. Speaking of, if we're building a monastery at St. Mary's – what's a monastery without a brewery?"

"That's like some true blue Holy Spirit talking right there, man." Isherwood was smiling and nodding. His head jerked to the side suddenly, distracted by a thought. He held up a finger and walked away mumbling about the *Teenage Mutant Ninja Turtles*.

"Man," Patrick was saying, as Padre joined him in a massive storage closet along the armory's back wall. He was looking up at a two-story mountain of white plastic 20-gallon buckets filled with rice and grains. "That's a lot of gumbo."

Padre was laughing. "Look at these," he said, opening another bucket full of vacuum-sealed seed packets.

"Whoa, Father." Patrick said, turning in the priest's direction. "That's like the most BA apocalypse uniform I've ever seen."

"Cowabunga, dudes!" Isherwood said, smiling like an idiot from the other side of the doorway. Copying Padre, he had found a double back harness for the katana samurai swords he had found earlier. He had taken the Howard Clark and the World War II Showa-period swords, leaving the third one for another day.

"Leonardo, right?" Justin said, walking up from behind. "I can respect that. Just please never say 'totally tubular'. Okay, turtle power?"

After another hour or so of work, they had loaded up the additional munitions and added some additional rations to their supplies. They had also carried out the surprisingly ferocious girl. Miraculously, Padre had succeeded in getting her to eat and drink something, but the momentary armistice ended quickly. She started lunging at them, snapping her teeth like one of the undead. She actually tore a piece out of Marshall's shirt. Regretfully, they ended up strapping her to an ironing board and gagging her. They laid her in the bed of the troop transport.

Padre asked for a moment with her and also asked for Isherwood to join him. The priest brought a small book out from the folds of his cassock and began praying over the girl. From another pocket, he brought out a small bottle of holy water. He asked Isherwood to get out the rosary that he knew Isherwood kept in his pocket and to pray it beside him. Isherwood realized soon thereafter that Padre

15

was exorcising the little girl, or at least beginning to. They would repeat this procedure several times over the next couple of days.

"Alright, my brothers," Isherwood said when they had finished packing in the last load. "The next stop is Whiskey Bay, except I'd like to make one last pit stop on the way."

CHAPTER ONE: THE TOWER

Whiskey Bay was less than an hour's drive from the plantation home under pre-zombie conditions. It took the men considerably more time as many of the back roads they had chosen needed clearing. There were car wrecks *everywhere*.

The majority of Sara's family property lay directly south of Interstate 10. The interstate was mostly one long bridge through this particular stretch of southern Louisiana. There was a mainland portion of their property, but the larger part was called "the Island." It wasn't exactly island, but it was surrounded by the Atchafalaya River. The Atchafalaya curved around its western side, while a manmade pilot channel ran straight along its eastern side. The pilot channel was made to divert water from the Atchafalaya and provide a more navigable waterway. The river and the pilot channel re-converged at the southern end of the Island.

After a full day and a half of preparations, side trips, and back roads since leaving St. Mary's, they caught sight of smoke rising from the interstate. They had braved Highway 190 after leaving Livonia. This had been the only major road they had taken. They traveled west on it for around twelve miles. They had tried traveling on the Old Highway 190 which paralleled it for a couple miles, but the newer, straighter road proved to be the safer option. Old Blue was still at the head of their caravan and Patrick was driving it. Isherwood had instructed him to stop before any rise in the roadway. He was especially wary of road blocks and ambushes on the highway. Patrick would stop whenever his sight lines for the road ahead were obstructed to less than a half mile. When this happened, one vehicle – usually Isherwood in the Jeep – would scout ahead.

There was an orange flare gun in each vehicle's glove box. Thankfully, none were needed for their short trip down Highway 190. Even the wrecks in the road were easy enough to drive around. Isherwood found himself wishing that they would encounter *somebody* – there's just no way the pandemic was this widespread. *Just how rare had it been for them to survive?*

The caravan came to a full stop when the Krotz Springs double bridge appeared in the distance. It was a natural choke point. If some band of thugs wanted to set up a barricade, this would be the spot. They would not be crossing the bridge, but they would be in range of it as they veered south along the east bank of the Atchafalaya River. From here, they would be taking 975, the river road that followed along the Atchafalaya south through the Sherburne Wildlife Management Area and Atchafalaya National Wildlife Refuge, or at least what used to be refuges.

"Nah, I can't see anything, either." Justin said, looking through the scope of a rifle he'd laid across the hood of the modified Cadillac Escalade he was driving.

Isherwood nodded and lifted his face from his own scope. "Alright, good enough for me."

"Glad we're not going through Krotz Springs," Patrick said, getting back in Old Blue. "Place never felt right. Speed trap and all."

"They were all bad along this stretch." Justin agreed. "Wouldn't mind just hauling butt over that bridge and through town going around ninety or a hundred, just cause."

"Maybe next time?" Isherwood asked, closing the Jeep door without waiting for an answer. The rest of them followed suit. As expected, they encountered no resistance as they turned off Highway 190 and onto 975. The biggest obstacle they encountered in the mostly deserted wildlife refuge was a buck chasing a doe across the roadway. They ran right out the woods towards the Pilot Channel, passing inches in front of the giant grill of the troop transport vehicle. Marshall slammed on the brakes and Padre nearly rear-ended the transport. The deer barely noticed as they swept through.

*****

The caravan parked in the middle of gravel roadway beside a cell phone tower. The vehicles formed a diamond pattern around the large Army transport truck they had liberated from the National Guard armory nearly a week ago. Old Blue parked out front, as always, while Isherwood's Jeep and Justin's Escalade parked on either side of the transport truck. Padre parked behind the transport in the Humvee.

Marshall got out of the transport and switched positions with Isherwood, getting into the Jeep. Isherwood closed the driver's side door and left the Jeep. He walked up to the gate of the chain-link fence that surrounded the base of the cell phone and radio tower. They were still about a mile north of I-10 and only slightly northeast of the camp where Glenn and the rest of Sara's family were trapped.

They were in the middle of the Sherburne Wildlife Management Area. *Just the right spot,* Isherwood thought to himself, *for a massive cell phone tower.* The tower was massive. Standing at the gate, Isherwood looked up at it, shielding his eyes from the bright sky. He had read on the various maps he'd managed to put together that the tower rose over 150 feet.

Isherwood left the gate and walked back over to the Jeep. He opened the back tailgate to retrieve the set of bolt cutters. "Padlock?" Justin asked from the turret of the Escalade.

"Yeah," Isherwood answered. "Thank God, too. I didn't want to be climbing over that razor wire."

"Yeah, buddy. It's up to you to repopulate the earth."

"You okay climbing that thing?" Padre asked.

Isherwood tried putting on a nonchalant ain't-no-thing face, but gave up. "Yup. Got to. We talked about it, and I'm the only one that has the slightest chance of recognizing the landmarks from up there. None of y'all have ever even been to the camp, except you, Justin, and that was only once. I'm not gonna lie – y'all better grab your umbrellas, because that's not gonna be rain that comes sprinkling down. It's gonna be my *pee*. My knees are already all wibbly-wobbily."

After about another half an hour, Isherwood clipped his harness to the ladder at over one hundred feet. He had climbed as high as his knees would let him. Even though he was tied off, he kept one gloved hand gripped tight to the ladder. He turned ever so slightly and caught a stiff wind. He flung his free hand back to the rung of the ladder. After a moment and a couple more "Hail Marys," he again let his left hand drop down again. He slowly turned to face Interstate 10 at his back.

The interstate stretched for miles and miles, from horizon to horizon. He couldn't believe how high one hundred and fifty feet had taken him into the air. He felt like he could see clear to Texas on a clear day. Isherwood figured he must be five times as high as the St. Mary's bell tower. He was almost as high as the tops of the towers supporting the Audubon Bridge, which they had led the long snake of zombies across just over a week ago. *Had it been only a week?*

His stomach lurched as he thought about how high he was. He pushed the contents of his stomach back down and forced his swirling vision to clear. He dared not look directly down beyond his feet. What he saw stretching out behind him was enough.

Isherwood had thought he'd seen just about as many zombies as a person *could* see. He had been so wrong. From the crew he'd led across the bridge to Pickett's charge at the levee to, just a day or so ago, the swarm coming out of the spillway, he must have dealt with at least five thousand by now. But there were still so many more below him.

As he looked down now, he couldn't believe the wreckage contained in just one thin strip of roadway. Thin strands of smoke were rising diagonally into the sky from charred wrecks. After all this time, the smoke was still rising. Isherwood could even see flames still spilling out of cars along the roadway. He thought maybe one burned into the next, like a long fuse running all the way to Lafayette or Baton

Rouge. The cities sat on either horizon. Thick smoke hung like black shrouds over both of them.

He was still quite a distance from the interstate. He squinted, but still couldn't see any sign of the undead. There was something odd about the roadway, though, like the hazy mirage that hangs around a gasoline fire. There was a strange sort of movement along the roadway. He put his binoculars up to his eyes, but he still couldn't make anything out except for the small lumps of cars – but wait. As his eyes adjusted, he began to understand what he was seeing.

It was like the videos he'd seen of the ocean floor, where endless fields of kelp or seagrass or whatever just drifted back and forth moved by unseen currents.

He could see the tops of the cars like flat squares, but not the sides.

The realization of what he was seeing struck him like a thunder bolt. The funny movement was them, moving listlessly side to side. They were just standing and waiting, some of them. Others seemed to be slowly groping their way toward one horizon or the other. Some seemed to be just drifting back and forth, as though first pulled toward the flames of Lafayette then slowly being distracted backward by Baton Rouge burning. Maybe it was the vibrations of explosions carried along the roadway that drew them first in one direction and then the other, alternating endlessly. They were completely filling the interstate like a slow-moving river pressing past and submerging the endless lines of cars and trucks like small islands in the stream.

He was not downwind of them, thankfully, nor even upwind, if that even mattered, but he could still hear the moans. They were not the excited moans that would rise from their rotting throats when living flesh was in sight. The moans were vast, however. It sounded like a giant, bored pipe organ made up of a thousand, thousand throats. It was horrifying, too.

Isherwood tried pulling his eyes away from the terrible scene. He eventually forced his eyes to scan the roadway up and down for exit ramps, especially directly behind him to the Whiskey Bay ramp. When he finally spotted it, he could see only the leading edge of it. But he could see enough. There was general, though still aimless, movement towards and leading down into the ramp. The river of zombies was narrowed there to thin rivulets where the cars were crammed too tight for zombies to pass abreast. No, it wasn't that the cars were crammed so much as – Isherwood blinked at the sight and felt his stomach lurch. Rotting flesh, scratched and torn from a thousand passing bodies was gradually damming up the exit ramp.

It didn't matter, though. Isherwood could see the zed heads spilling over the sides of the roadway. He couldn't see where they fell. The tree tops blocked that. He was pretty sure, though, that they just got right back up again.

Isherwood estimated that there were maybe two to three thousand per mile. *God, where had they all come from?* If they started shooting at any point along the roadway, they would merely break the dam at that point. The dead would eventually start raining down on them. It might only be a trickle at first as the dead slowly surged against maybe one hundred feet of roadway. They would eventually mound up, Isherwood imagined, against the sides of the roadway, maybe across the whole width of the road. The dead would start using the still-squirming mounds below them as a ramp. The river of dead would flow, then, up and over the sides of the roadway. The whole river would start spilling down over the sides of the road, right down on them.

He realized that Sara's family was lucky to be surrounded by *only* a few thousand. Any intrusion by their own rescue party would likely only add to these numbers. And by quite a lot.

"My God," he finally said to himself, lowering the binoculars. "What the *hell* are we gonna do?"

CHAPTER TWO:

PLAN CHICKEN

"Well?" Patrick asked, as Isherwood emerged from inside the chain link enclosure at the bottom of the cell phone tower. They were several new corpses littering the roadway. Besides fending off the low to moderate concentration of zombies, they had all been watching as their friend climbed up the tower and as he stared into the distance southward. Even from all the way on the ground, they could tell that Isherwood had not liked what he'd seen.

Dropping the pretense of their defensive position, they had grouped around Isherwood's Jeep, as he walked back to it in silence.

"That bad, huh?" Marshall asked.

"Yup," Isherwood said finally. "*That* bad."

"Like *how* bad?" Justin asked. "Are we talking thousands? Tens of thousands? Millions?"

"My guess is that if we started shooting at the exit ramps we'd probably drawn in fifty, maybe sixty, thousand before it was all over – one way or the other. The Interstate looks like it's clogged almost solid between Lafayette and Baton Rouge."

The men reacted in different ways. Patrick threw his head back, letting it loll back and forth between his shoulders. Justin actually bent over and put his head between his legs. Father Simeon may have blinked.

"There's just no passing the exit ramps that lead from I-10 to the mainland part of Whiskey Bay." Isherwood concluded.

Patrick was squinting at him with a look of confusion on his face. "I thought you said Sara's family were trapped on the Island part of Whiskey Bay, not the mainland side. Why would we even try to come up on the mainland side?"

"One option we had," Isherwood explained, "was entrenching near the exit ramps and using our seventy-five-yard strategy to build up a corpse wall of such enormous height that we'd clear the whole area of zeds."

"Wait," Marshall said. "You're saying the camp is on the *other* side of the Atchafalaya? Clearing out this side of the river wouldn't do nothing to help those folks, am I right? What am I missing?"

"Those things," Padre interjected. "Once they start moaning, they draw others in for miles and miles. It's conceivable that our gun fire would draw the zombies away from the camp, allowing Sara's family to escape. They'd be lured towards us, but would probably just get swept up, harmlessly, into the Pilot Channel and never even make it to us."

They were all quiet for a moment mulling this over. "So," Isherwood continued. "Our other option would be crossing the Pilot Channel between I-10 and where the Pilot Channel branches off from the Atchafalaya. We could entrench somewhere north of I-10 and that would bring the hoard spilling off I-10 towards us, as well as drawing the rest of the zeds on the Island to us."

Justin was nodding. "But the downside of Plan B would be –"

"We leave the vehicles behind," Isherwood answered.

"Right." Justin said, sighing.

"And Plan C?" Patrick asked.

"Plan C would be backtracking to Krotz Springs and sticking to the western bank of the Atchafalaya. We'd have the vehicles, which is good, but I just don't think we'd be close enough to I-10 to lure enough zeds toward us and into the Atchafalaya. Of course, the zeds probably wouldn't get anywhere near us. The flow of the Atchafalaya would push them right back against the northern end of the Island. But I just don't think this approach would work fast enough. The camp's been out of food for two days now. We could also float down one side of the Island or the other and attack from the south of I-10 but that would likely mean we'd be drawing thousands of zeds past their camp."

"Are they – Sara's family – expecting us to follow one of these plans in particular?" Padre asked.

Isherwood shook his head. "We discussed the options, but they knew we'd have to assess the situation before we could pick a route."

"What're you, thinking, old man?" Marshall asked Isherwood. Marshall was actually at least a decade older than Isherwood.

"Well," he said, taking a deep breath. "I'm thinking we ditch the vehicles and go with Plan B, because I'm itching to get on the Island."

"But wouldn't that leave us surrounded by a wall of corpses?" Patrick asked. "We'd have to scramble over the top and probably get munched on in the process or worse – get stuck under an avalanche of gore."

"You know," Padre said, raising the forefinger of his right hand. His head was lowered in thought. "There is another way. All these ideas have us attacking from land. What if we stayed in the water?"

"Like an amphibious assault?" Isherwood asked skeptically.

Padre shook his head. "No, what if we stayed put in the water? I'm thinking the Pilot Channel over the Atchafalaya. We could lay anchor, hopefully in the middle of the channel, and draw them in with gunfire or whatever – maybe the flares."

Isherwood was now smiling broadly. "Heck yes! Brillant, Father. This is like an idea I had for floating chicken farms. The idea was to draw the River Dead back into the water once the river had belched them up onto the shore."

"Uhhh," Padre was frowning in confusion. "I guess – yeah, but we're the chickens in this scenario."

"Speak for yourself, Father." Justin interrupted.

Padre just ignored the remark. "We'd need to find a couple boats and load them up with ammo. We'd want to lay anchor upstream of the I-10 bridge, too, I'm thinking. They'll start dumping into the river from the shores and probably float by us without getting close, but the ones dropping from the I-10 bridge might swarm the boat like ants in a flood *if* we're downstream of the bridge."

"Perfect." Isherwood said. "Y'all in? I think I saw a sign back up the road by the park shooting range that pointed to a boat launch and landing. I bet the park rangers have a few boats tied up there."

"I like it. *A lot.*" Patrick said. "I've been having nightmares of sinking into a sea of corpses and zombies. Like when Kevin Arnold sank into that pit of candy in *The Wonder Years* – y'all remember that? No? Okay. Nevermind. But yeah, I'm in."

"Me, too." Marshall added. "I like it. I'm pretty good with a boat, too."

"Me three, or – well, five, actually." Justin added. "*Whatever*, sounds good. Plan 'C' for 'chicken.'"

*****

They parked along 975, which was actually called the Whiskey Bay Highway. They left the vehicles in the same diamond formation as they had at the cell phone tower. They locked the troop transport with the little girl still inside. They left her still strapped the ironing board, but they took out her gag and released one of her arms. They left food and water within her reach and prayed they'd return, at least for her sake.

They never even attempted the five or so miles back to the docks that Isherwood thought he had seen by the Sherburne WMA Shooting Range. Before they got there, they realized that there was a solid mile or so of fishing camps along the eastern bank of the Pilot Channel, itself. These camps were just close enough to the interstate that any noise, even the quietest of generators, would have drawn in swarms of the undead. Either they had all been abandoned early on, or the swarms had come and gone. The camps all appeared now to be deserted, but the men were extremely wary nonetheless.

Isherwood and Marshall left to scout for boats, while the remaining three started organizing the gear for transfer onto the boats.

"Oh man," Isherwood said to Marshall. He had a pretty good view before leaving the road of the channel beyond the camps. "I was thinking these camps would have piers. You know, something for the boats to be tied to, and we'd just have to untie and go."

"Nope." Marshall said, matter-of-factly. "I bet the current's just too strong 'round here. Boats would just slam into the piers. Both'd get pretty messed up."

"Channel might be deeper than I was thinking, too."

"Well, yeah, but even so, they could pontoon a pier – hey, now." Marshall broke off and pointed. "There's a pretty girl right there."

As they rounded the first camp they came to, they saw a large sport fishing boat sitting on a trailer in dry dock. The dry dock consisted of a simple aluminum carport-like structure.

"You think we'll be able to launch her right here? Just back the trailer into the water?" Isherwood asked.

"I wouldn't under normal circumstances, but ain't nothing normal about nothing anymore. I 'magine that motor will start drawing the creatures in pretty fast. If not, we can go up the road a piece to a launch."

"You know of—?" Isherwood made to reply but was interrupted by the sudden look of fear spreading across Marshall's face.

"Head's up!" Marshall cried drawing his pistol.

Isherwood spun in place, somehow managing to push Marshall's arm down so he lowered the gun. He pulled out one of the katanas from the double sheath harness on his back. The motion of bringing the sword over his head to unsheathe it was perfect. He continued the motion downward, bringing the blade down with both hands. The katana sliced through the skull of a zombie diagonally. The creature fell to its knees before Isherwood, as though kneeling in homage to the blade.

"Oh, wow." Isherwood whispered. "I barely felt the blade make impact. That's just – wow." He stammered relaxing the long handle of the sword in his grip.

"Yeah, well. Thanks for not cutting my head off while you were swinging that thing." Marshall grumbled, as he looked over the body of the decapitated zombie.

"Sorry about that. I didn't want the report of the pistol to draw anymore in, you know?"

"Would'ya lookey here?" Marshall said. He had taken something out of the zombie's pockets. It was a set of keys on a little chain attached to a red float. "Looks like we've met the proprietor of this 'ere establishment." Marshall said smiling, as the keys twinkled back and forth between his fingertips. "Why don't you go ahead and take care of those fellas – the neighbors, probably – while I take a look-see around the boat?"

"What?" Isherwood burst out. He whirled back around in tacit acceptance of Marshall's plan. He had been so absorbed in the power of the katana blade that he hadn't noticed the small group of zombies staggering toward them.

"Alright. Okay, let's do this." Isherwood said. He squared up his feet in what he thought he remembered was the right stance for the sword. He bent his knees and aimed his body perpendicular to the oncoming zombies. He raised the sword behind his head and readied himself to bring it down onto the next skull. He practiced pivoting at his waist for extra strength.

A blood-stained beard hung from the mangled jaw bone of the first zombie. Isherwood made the mistake of looking into the creature's yawning mouth instead of his target. The small distraction brought the blade streaking through the creature's mouth. Isherwood was yanked from his feet as the blade came to a sudden halt as it embedded halfway into the creature's skull.

"Ah, crap." Isherwood's eyes were darting back and forth as the zombies began to flank him. He released his grip on the priceless katana and reached for the second sword sheathed across his back. He realized he had been overthinking the blade – the first, perfect swing had been on instinct. *But how do I purposely revert to instinct?* He asked himself. Fortunately, the needs of the present quickly cleared his mind.

The bearded zombie still stood in the middle of the oncoming crowd. He looked like a ghastly version of Pinocchio with the blade jutting out from his skull right under the nose. Inadvertently, Pinocchio was diverting the flow of zombies toward Isherwood into two streams. The two streams were surrounding him.

Isherwood backpedaled out of the inadvertent pincer attack of the oncoming zombies. He strafed to one side of the crowd, and attacked the nearest zombie from its flank. It was a teenage girl wearing just a long t-shirt that read "Grumpy" and depicted the cartoon dwarf. She had apparently been attacked in the night while still wearing her pajamas.

Isherwood aimed this time for the back of the creature's slender neck. A thought rattled around somewhere in his head. He knew slicing right between the cervical vertebrae of the neck was really difficult, but maybe the katana would slice through the bone just as easily as the gaps between. Slicing through an inch or so of vertebrae had to be easier than slicing through an entire skull, he thought. *Right?*

Grumpy's head was flying through the air before Isherwood even realized that he'd made impact. He nodded in satisfaction. He began circling around the oncoming hoard. Heads began flying here and there. Pinocchio was still wobbling on his feet at the center of the maelstrom, turning as Isherwood revolved around him. He was jerking the blade, which was still protruding several feet out of his skull, as he turned. From above, the scene looked like a massive clock, advancing erratically through the hours.

Despite the clock, Isherwood had sliced through the entire company of zombies in under a minute. When it was nearly over, he strode back over to Pinocchio and wrapped his hand around the hilt of the katana. He felt like a whole different swordsman since trapping the blade in the creature's skull. Still holding the sword, he reared back and simultaneously kicked out, planting the sole of his boot across the creature's chest. The zombie was thrown backward. Isherwood watched as the creature sprawled backward onto the ground. He was standing now with a sword in each hand.

He remembered suddenly the scene when Maximus pulled two Gladius swords from the chest of an enemy and then decapitated him with them like hedge clippers. He started reciting to himself as he advanced on the zombie, "My name is Maximus Decimus Meridius, Commander of the armies of the North, General of the Felix legions, loyal servant to the true emperor – Ah hell, nevermind." He sheathed the sword he had retrieved and sliced through Pinocchio's neck with the remaining katana. "Don't get cocky, kid." He said to himself, remembering a particularly bad paper cut he'd given himself just the day before.

*****

Isherwood had continued clearing the area of zombies. He worked his way through the yards of the two neighboring camps and found himself back on the road. There, his path intersected with Padre's. The priests was keeping a low profile along the roadway. Fortunately, the road curved not far from their position. They would have been much more visible on an open roadway. The few moans the zombies had made, however, before Padre could dispatch them would likely draw more in. Their time was running short.

"Ready for Plan Chicken?" Isherwood asked as he came across the priest. Padre answered with a rolling nod and a thumbs up. Before either could say anything else, their heads turned abruptly back to the first camp, to the sound of a boat motor. Marshall had the motor running. After letting it run a couple minutes, he let it throttle back down and switched it off.

"I've been thinking, Padre." Isherwood said as they jogged back along the road. "That Pilot Channel – it's got a pretty strong current at the center and deep, too. A normal anchoring might not work. We might have to think of other options, or at least not anchor right in the middle. Last thing we want is to start slipping under that bridge and the zombies start dropping on our heads at thirty or forty feet."

The priest nodded, considering this. "Maybe we make sure we've got some extra rope *and* – doesn't one of the trucks have a grappling hook launcher?"

Before Isherwood could respond, they ran into Justin and Patrick. "Not much going in the way of zombies back the other way," Justin said. "How 'bout y'all?"

"Getting a little thick," Isherwood said, taking a moment to wipe the blood from his blade before re-sheathing it. "Sounds like ol' Marshall got us a ride."

Padre disappeared and reappeared holding a little case that held one of the Army-issue LGHs and some extra rope. They all grabbed or two of the bags of ammo and supplies Patrick had put together for the boat. "Jeez, Patrick." Justin complained. "You pack like my wife. I thought this was just going to be a three-hour tour, Gilligan!"

"Just the essentials," Patrick smiled.

"Think we can launch the boat right here?" Isherwood asked them as they walked under the little roof that the boat was stored under.

"Maybe," Marshall answered appearing from inside the cabin of the sport fishing boat. "Can one of y'all wade out into the water to check the depth?"

"Don't think we'll have the time," Patrick said pointing back up the road-way. They all looked. They could see between the two neighboring camps and through to the road as it curved away to the south. A sizeable crowd of zombies had emerged, drawn either by the moans of their brethren or the sound of the boat motor.

"Alright," Marshall said. The sound of panic was audible in his voice, though still far off. "Y'all knock away those blocks behind the tires of the trailer. We'll roll her right in. The trailer will just have to take care of itself."

After throwing their bags of gear haphazardly into the boat, they began pushing the trailer backward toward the water. There was only a slight slope and not much of a bank. It look like the trailer would just roll backward without much issue. "You released all the straps, right?" Isherwood asked Marshall.

"Yup, nothing keeping this boat on this trailer but gravity." Marshall nod-ded. "Ought to float right off. Trailer will get pretty moist, though, I'd imagine."

"Crap!" Patrick said, pointing to the oncoming zombies. He was struggling with the others to both push the trailer backward and push in down, keeping it level and balanced. "They're spilling down the little hill coming off the road. Coming faster."

The back half of the trailer was now cantilevered over the water. The wheels of the trailer finally rolled into the water, and they found that the bank started dropping off precipitously. The trailer started rolling on its own without needing to be pushed, and the four men started slipping against the wet grass of the bank chasing after the trailer. The grass quickly turned into slick mud.

"Whoa-ho, guys." Marshall yelled. "Jus' let her go. Let her do her thing."

Whether they wanted to or not, they had to let the trailer go. Justin slid onto his back into the water, though he only sank a few feet. The trailer quickly disappeared into the depths of the water. They saw it turn a bit into the current before it disappeared altogether. The boat bobbed a little, but slid right out into open water. Marshall went to the motor to crank it back up again before it was lost to the current.

Just as Marshall started turning the ignition key in the crew quarters, Justin felt a tug on his leg below the waterline. He was still laying on his back, with just his head and kneecaps sticking out of the water. "Ah, hell!" He yelled, trying to crawl backwards out of the water.

A head burst out from the water between Justin's legs. The flesh as well as water was dripping from the zombie's water-logged face. Putrid water poured from its open mouth, as it gurgled a choked and soggy moan. A hand reached out to Justin's face. The flesh was almost entirely rotted off. The fingers were just bare phalange bones.

BLLLARRONNG!! A shot rang out, briefly quieting the splashing water and oncoming moans. Isherwood looked back to see Padre standing at the bank with smoke rising from the rifle he had pulled from across his back. "Nice, Padre!" Isherwood called out. Padre just nodded and re-slung the rifle into its harness.

Justin was still scrambling backward and onto the bank. The others were getting ready to wade towards the boat, assuming Marshall could get it back to them. "Whoa, whoa, whoa –!" Justin was stammering. "Wait – hey! Don't go in there. There were other hands. Other things scratching at me."

"Maybe so, but we ain't got much of a choice. Look." Isherwood answered pointing backward. There were about twenty or thirty zombies within ten yards of the bank, and possibly a hundred more pressing in behind them.

"Screw that." Justin said, looking around madly. "You don't get it. Look – get in *that.* Over there!" He was pointing to a little flat-bottomed piroque boat. It had no motor, but there was a paddle, possibly. "Don't get too close, Marshall!" Justin was yelling at the boat beginning to work its way back upstream.

The piroque was half-submerged along the other end of the property, near the property line with the neighbor. The men made a break for it as the line of zombies closed in. They turned it over. Padre was muttering a prayer or blessing, probably that the boat had no leaks.

Isherwood was the last to get on board. He pushed them off into the water. He didn't look back, but looking forward all the rifles and pistols seemed to be aimed at him. He tried keeping his eyes open as they opened fire. They were aiming all around him, but it felt like a firing line. He thought Justin might've even been aiming between Isherwood's legs. He fought hard against instinct to lunge toward the gunfire, but he couldn't. He lost his footing and tripped towards the boat. His head hit the side of the boat. Bewildered, he regained consciousness choking on a mouthful of water. He felt hands pulling at him from opposite directions. He hoped to God that the right direction won.

Eventually, Isherwood opened his eyes to the blue sky. He was lying face up along the bottom of the boat, but there was water sloshing against the sides of his head. He was alternately deafened, one ear at a time, as the water lolled back and force. He could hear Justin's and Patrick's voices. They were speaking calmly, and he was instantly reassured.

He sat upright at the bottom of the boat, rubbing his head. He immediately noticed that the water he had been lying in – it was just a little too deep for the sake of comfort. Patrick was doing his best with the oar, but they had been taken swiftly into the current. He saw, too, that the other boat was not far off now. He could hear Marshall shouting instructions now. He tapped the water from his ear canals and could hear even better.

"Y'all be quick," Marshall was saying. "When I bring her in, the swell of water will likely capsize that little guy, especially seeing as how it's half-sunk already."

"Alright, we got it." Patrick answered back. "Ish, you got all that?"

Isherwood squinted towards what he thought was Patrick and nodded. He began shifting his legs into a squatting position. Padre was up and over the side of the larger boat before Isherwood even realized the boat was close enough. The priest had no problem with the climb despite the long black cassock. The rifles stayed secured in their holsters at his back.

Justin and Patrick guided Isherwood as he grabbed the railing of the fishing boat. They helped boost him up and over. The upward pressure brought water spilling over the sides of the piroque. They jumped up together against the side of the boat. Isherwood tumbled over onto the deck, while Padre helped pull Justin and Patrick up into the boat.

As they all sat huddled and catching their breath on the deck of the boat, squeezing in between the heavy sacks of ammo and supplies, they were watching the short stretch of shoreline they had just narrowly escaped from. The swarm of zombies was rushing headlong into the water after them. They seemed completely unaware of the water. Their eyes never wavered from the men and the boat, even as they slipped under the water. The water by the shore also seemed unaware of the rush of walking corpses. It wasn't churning, as with a hoard of swimmers rushing off the beach. The water was unnaturally still. Soon, there would be no sign at all of what lay beneath the surface.

CHAPTER THREE: THE BRIDGE

The Interstate 10 bridge soon loomed overhead. It stood large on the horizon as soon as they turned their attention away from the shoreline, where the zombies were still spilling into the water after them.

"Does this thing have a horn on it? Like a foghorn or something?" Isherwood asked. He had quickly forgotten the blow to his head, even though a lump was steadily swelling from his scalp. As he watched the zombies spilling into the water after him, he again felt the rush of anxiety for his in-laws. Though they were only in-laws, they were family to him. Now that the rescue party had arrived, more or less, he was itching to sound the trumpets and relieve the siege. He smiled, whispering to himself that *the cavalry had arrived.*

"Be my guest," Marshall answered from the captain's seat behind the wheel. "I think it's that one," he said pointing to a switch on the console just under the marine compass.

"Sweet," Isherwood smiled. "Let's get this thing started." He looked ahead to the bridge so he could watch the reaction of the zombies to the horn. Even before he flipped the switch, he saw the silhouette of a body tumbling over the side of the bridge. He flipped the switch.

The horn sounded small as it echoed across the rumbling Pilot Channel. It was little more than a car horn. It did the trick, though. More bodies started falling over the side of the bridge.

"Man, we need something louder than that, right?" Patrick was asking from the afterdeck.

"How about some live bait?" Isherwood mumbled as he climbed the ladder to the fishing tower about the cabin. Holding onto the rail, he started hollering and carrying on, beckoning the zombies to come to the boat.

"Hey, this oughta do the trick," Marshall said rummaging through the cabinets inside the cabin. Isherwood's screams were soon overwhelmed by a much louder blaring sound. Marshall had stepped out of the cabin to lean over the side rail of the boat.

Isherwood jumped at the sound of the fog horn, nearly losing his footing and falling from the platform. The fog horn echoed against the sides of the Pilot Channel and down the waterway, to the bridge and beyond. By the time Marshall had released the trigger, the sound of the moans was already gathering in strength. The thousands of zombies up and down the interstate moaned in reply. The sound of the horn was like a rock being thrown into the middle of a still pond. The moans rippled outward for miles.

"Wow." Isherwood said, climbing back down from the fishing tower. "That oughtta do it. Now, I sure hope we've got a good anchor or we just signed our own death warrant."

The four men all looked around. Confusion and then panic seized their faces. They could see no anchor.

"Anchor?" Marshall asked. "Oh yeah, that should be up there," he said, pointing forward. Sure enough, there was an anchor and a windlass mounted to the front deck of the boat. "Let me get a little closer to the bridge first. If we anchor here and slowly feed out line all the way to the bridge, this current might smack us from bank to bank."

"Oh yeah, just a little closer. No big." Justin said shaking his head. He was spinning back and forth in a vinyl chair mounted on the deck.

Isherwood climbed over to where the anchor was secured. He let out a big sigh of relief, and then tilted his head in thought. "Hey, this thing got a radio?" He said turning back to Marshall. The older man nodded and pointed to an area on the console just beside Isherwood's hand. "Oh," he said. "I see."

Isherwood turned his head to the others, but it was just Justin still sitting on the vinyl seat and Patrick rummaging through the supply bags. Padre had disappeared. "What the heck?" He said, dropping the radio handset and looking overboard.

"What?" Justin said, still swiveling in place. "Oh, Padre went below decks or whatever you say in ship jargon."

"Huh?" Isherwood said, looking at Justin like he was a mad man. "But this thing's too small for below—"

"Look through the little door there." Justin said pointing. The door was right beside Isherwood.

"What? How'd they get by me? I was right here."

"Dude, did you hit your head or something?" Justin said chuckling. He winked at Patrick.

"Yeah, actually."

"Why don't you come sit down, buddy." Justin said, standing up to give up his seat to Isherwood.

"Nah, that's okay. If it is a concussion, I better stay active. I'll stay over here with the radio. Can you or Patrick try contacting the camp with the portable radio? Or have you already done that and I missed it?"

"*Yeah*, we did that like five minutes ago, dude." Justin said, irritated. "Just kidding. You're not *that* far gone. Yeah, we'll help out with the radio."

"Good Lord," Patrick said, looking up from the bags. The other two turned to see Marshall climbing up onto the forward deck of the boat to drop the anchor. But that wasn't what Patrick was pointing at. The bridge was now only about two hundred yards away. They could see the zombies reaching for them from the bridge deck. They were in a frenzy, scrambling over the sides to get to them. They were falling into the channel now, dozens at a time. There was a steady stream of them falling over the side.

Isherwood caught a glimpse of one falling head first into the water. Though it was still too far away, he felt like he connected eyes with it for just a split second. Even as it fell, it was still reaching for him, completely oblivious to the water or the impact below.

Few resurfaced. There was no trail of zombies treading water as they were forced downstream. They appeared to just sink, as though weighted down. But on the far side of the bridge, the water became more turbulent. Clumps of zombies came roiling back up to the surface, only to re-submerge. The channel was washing away their filth and rot.

The zombies were filling the banks, as well. The undead were staggering straight down the bank into the water, just as they had where they had launched the boat.

"My God, it can't be this easy, can it?" Patrick asked.

"Dude!" Justin yelled indignantly. He threw an empty beer can at his friend, even as Padre re-emerged from below decks. "Don't say stuff like that. You'll jinx us."

Padre was admiring the scene, as well. His gaze drifted from the bridge down to Marshall. They were still edging closer and closer to the bridge. "Marshall?" Padre asked. "How's that anchor coming?"

"You see?" Justin said, cursing. "What'd I tell you? You hear Padre? He never says anything unless something terrible is happening. Now something's gonna happen. Mark it."

"S'all good," Marshall called back. He was beginning to crawl back across the forward deck to the cabin.

"Uh-huh." Patrick said, mocking Justin.

"Just saw the first tug on the anchor line." Marshall continued. "Hold on to something. The anchor's about to spin us around."

"Did he just say hold on?" Justin asked. "Yup, 'hold on,' he says. That's how it begins. Then there's yelling and *screaming*."

"You keeping the motors on through this?" Isherwood asked ignoring Justin. "Just idling?"

"Yeah, thought it'd be good to draw them in. And if'n we get in a jam, we can just drive back up the channel."

All went according to their plan. The just sat there watching the zombies hurtle themselves off the bridge. The original trickle of plummeting undead at the center of the bridge broadened across nearly the whole channel, as the oncoming throngs grew thicker and thicker. Zombies even came falling off the far side of the bridge, likely pushed off by the onslaught of undead pushing in from both directions.

After another half hour or so, Isherwood finally figured out he was trying to make contact with his in-laws' camp using a marine radio and not a CB. Luckily, the radio was a combination job. Marshall showed him how to switch frequencies, and within ten minutes, he'd made contact.

He heard a crackle of static on the radio and a fuzzy voice. After reporting his frequency, the voice on the other end grew much clearer. "Glenn? Is this Glenn? Missy? Over. *Click-shhh.*"

"This is Glenn, Isherwood. About time y'all showed up! *Click-shhh.*" At the sound of his voice, the others started hollering, excited that the other group was still alive.

"*So* glad to hear your voice, Mr. Glenn! How are the Z's at the camp? Over. *Click-shhh.*"

"Hey, whatever y'all're doing is working. They've started drifting off. We're almost to the point where we could clear them off ourselves. If we'd eaten, anyway. *Click-shhh.*"

"Roger that." Isherwood replied. "We'll keep it up for now. Maybe even until morning, depending on gas. Y'all gonna be able to meet us or do we need to come and get you? Over. *Click-shhh.*"

"I think y'all had better swing by the camp. *Click-shhh.*"

"Roger that. We'll hurry, okay? Over. *Click-shhh.*"

"Good. Please do." The radio stopped crackling and Glenn said no more.

"Dang." Isherwood said, shaking his head. "They didn't sound too good at all. There's gotta be a way I can just slip ashore with a pack of food without drawing attention. Bringing them to the channel would be a heck of a lot easier than vice-versa, right?"

"Look, man." Patrick said. "I get that you want to charge in, but we've got to stick together. We may need to carry some of them out on stretchers."

"We may need to *bury* some of them if I don't bring them some food." Isherwood shot back.

"Okay, let's think this through," Justin said. "You go in to deliver emergency food and then we follow you in once the zombies are cleared out. How do we find the camp? You're the only one that can get us there."

"That's no problem." Isherwood answered. "Glenn could give you directions from the Interstate."

"We don't want directions from the Interstate." Padre answered. "That's the last route we'd want to take inland."

"From the pipeline, then." Isherwood continued. "Just as good."

"Pipeline?" Patrick asked. "What pipeline?"

"That big ol' sucker on the far side of the bridge?" Marshall asked.

"That's the one," Isherwood answered. "Y'all see it, too?" He pointed to a two- or three-foot diameter pipe suspended about thirty feet from the water, about level with the bridge. Long cables ran from the pipe sections up to two tall towers on either bank. The towers rose high into the air, as tall or taller than the cell phone tower had been. From where the pipeline emerged from the ground on one side of the Pilot Channel to where it submerged on the Island, it likely stretched over a mile.

"You know," Isherwood said. "That pipeline gives me an idea. But it's — uh — dang, I can't believe I'm about to even suggest this."

"Go ahead, man." Patrick said. "You've had plenty of good ideas so far."

"All I'm gonna say is —" Justin also chimed in. "Fat boys don't do climbing, okay?"

Isherwood tilted his head at his friend, wondering how he had managed to anticipate his thinking. "That's it," he said, nodding. "Climbing. Padre, you brought that grappling hook, right?"

"Onto the pipeline, right?" Justin asked. "Look, dude. You're no Luke Sky-walker, ah-ight?"

"You're gonna shoot that grappling hook at an *oil* pipeline?" Marshall yelped.

"Wait," Padre said, holding up a hand. "This plan will involve us passing under the bridge, won't it?"

Isherwood nodded. "Right, Padre. We'd pull anchor and let the current take us just downstream of the pipeline. We'll reset the anchor down there. You or whoever shoots that grappling hook up to the pipeline, and I shimmy up with a pack of food. If I stay low to the pipeline, it'll be pretty easy — not like walking a tightrope or something."

Patrick was shaking his head. "But what about climbing from the rope to the pipeline? None of what you're describing is easy — not even for somebody who's trained on that stuff. *Especially* over water."

Padre was also shaking his head. "I don't like it," he said definitively. "Besides, it's unnecessary just yet. Give it at least another couple hours before you — before we — take a risk like that. The shoreline might start to clear up, and then we could just park the boat and all go. Besides, just knowing we're here is something.

We've given the folks up at the camp hope, and that should give us at least another couple hours."

*****

So that was what they did. They waited in the fishing boat another hour or so. The current batted them back and forth across the middle of the Pilot Channel, but the anchor held. It was an effortless way of removing the zombie threat. The waterfall of zombies off the bridge continued unabated. Thousands of zombies were falling into the river from the bridge every hour.

The men's necks soon tired of looking up to the bridge to watch wave after wave of the undead falling down. Their eyes drifted down to the water level. There, they couldn't help but return the stares of the zombies. They were still reaching for them as they plummeted into the water, and doubtless were *still* reaching even while being churned into the depths below.

Despite the constant carnage, the shorelines never seemed to run out of zombies advancing heedless into the current. Isherwood was beginning to wonder if his initial assessment of the number of zombies had been accurate. They just might be facing the full combined population of Baton Rouge and Lafayette.

Since the anchor was mounted on the forward section of the boat, the boat had rotated into the current. The front of the boat was now facing upstream, and Marshall was still sitting in the captain's chair inside the boat's open air cabin. He was dutifully checking the boat every couple minutes or so, while the rest sat transfixed staring at the undead masses marching towards them and dropping into the water.

The boat's inboard motors were idling softly. They were ready, if needed, to be fired up at a moment's notice. The fuel gauge, too, was holding steady above half a tank. Marshall frowned, though, as he checked the anchor mount and the line that disappeared into the water. He leaned over the starboard side of the boat a bit to get a better angle on the anchor line. "What the—?" He mumbled.

The others made no sign of having heard him. Justin was actually below-decks taking a nap. The older man climbed through the narrow space between the cabin and the forward deck. He steadied himself by clutching to the small hatch on the deck that led to the hold below. He could actually feel the hatch door rattling softly as Justin snored below.

"Ah, *cat piss.*" He cursed. "Looks like we got a nibble," he yelled back to the men at back of the boat. Padre turned at the sound, but Isherwood and Patrick were on the brink of dozing off. Padre raised himself into a crouch and put his rosary back into his pocket.

The anchor line was moving oddly, more like a fishing line. Marshall reached out his arm to grab hold of it. He thought maybe he could slam it a couple of times against the side of the boat to knock off whatever was dragging against it.

He thought it might be a submerged log getting slowly wound up into the line. He probably should have considered other possibilities.

Marshall tugged on the line, drawing in some of the anchor line. He reached down along the waterline to pick up the slack. The water seethed as the current pushed against the side of the boat. The wash of bubbles hid the shadow that was rising out of the depths.

The older man howled as a hand suddenly emerged from the water and grabbed his wrist. He was already unbalanced as he had been reaching for the line. The pull against his wrist, though clumsy and groping, was enough for him to lose his balance completely.

Marshall slipped over the side of the boat just as Padre was rushing in to grab him. Padre was too late, but Marshall's hand was still clinging to the anchor line. As he fell, his hand twisted into the line. He was caught. In better conditions, he may have been relieved to avoid drowning. As it was, he had no chance.

Other shadows swarmed up the line. Faces appeared in the water. Marshall howled in pain as his lower body was ripped apart. The water reddened. There were only three, maybe four, zombies that came up along the line, but they moved like ants over a carcass. Padre tried pulling his friend and parishioner back into the boat, but it was too late. It had been too late as soon as he hit the water. Whether it had been the zombies or the anchor line tightening around him, he was gone below the waist.

The others arrived in time to see Marshall let go of Padre's hand and disappear into the water. It had all happened in just seconds.

Padre just lay still on the deck, as though he was still reaching for Marshall. The others let him be. The zombies had no way of climbing onto the boat, and they believed they were in no immediate danger. At least, they did for a couple more minutes.

CHAPTER FOUR:

THINGS FALL APART

They felt the pull of the current first. They never heard the line snap. It was probably cut far below the waterline by a zombie chewing at the moving line or drawn by Marshall's blood stains.

However it happened, they were nearly beneath the bridge before one of them thought to rev up the boat motor. By that time, fighting against the current to drive upstream would have trapped them under the falling dead.

All of a sudden, they heard the terrible heavy thuds of bodies falling across the decks and the roof of the tower.

"Just let 'er drift past the bridge," Isherwood called out as he unsheathed a single blade. There was just not enough room to even try to use both blades on the boat. They were floating backwards, but the current was gradually turning them broadsides. Despite the distractions, Isherwood saw that, if they were still broadsides at the wrong point when floating under the bridge and against the pilings, there was a very real chance of capsizing the boat. "Padre!" He yelled. "Help rotate us around to face forward when we pass those pilings. Push off against them."

Despite his grief, Padre had got back up. He was still on the forward deck. He would easily get knocked off balance if tried standing, so he knelt there. The rifles across his back were sort of a liability in his present predicament. Even the pair of .44s had enough kick to send him over the side if he wasn't careful. Or worse, he might punch a hole through the boat.

The zombies were raining down mostly feet first. They could hear their shin and calf bones cracking as they landed. Isherwood felt his blood chill. Despite bones visibly protruding from their legs, they kept coming.

All of a sudden, there were five surrounding Isherwood and Patrick on the aft deck. Some were crawling around the deck, snapping at their ankles. "Don't shoot down into the boat!" Isherwood called as he saw Patrick put his Glock to the temple of one of the ankle-biters. "The knife – use your knife!"

Even as he was saying it, Isherwood stabbed one of the zombies through the chest. He leveraged the sword against the zombie's spine and tipped it over the boat rail. He did this twice more, while Patrick went about stabbing the crawlers through their temples. There was so little room to move around the back of the boat that they were soon stepping on the creatures. A sickening, fetid liquid was soon sloshing back and forth in the boat.

Padre had pivoted around so that his back was against the windshield of the cabin. Somehow, despite the narrow space across the forward deck, three zombies were crawling after him. He'd already knocked two off the side. He was just trying to get them off of him, so he could push against the bridge pilings. The boat was already beginning to tip heavily backwards against the oncoming current.

Father Simeon used the imbalance against his attackers. He had stabilized his position by holding onto the metal railings on either side of the boat's windshield. He kicked at their faces with his boots. He was lucky to have worn heavy, high black boots beneath his cassock. He freed one hand from the railings and unholstered one of his .44s just as he placed a boot square against the chest of one of the zombies. Pushing the thing's torso up and backward, he fired at close range and blew the creature's head off. Its body slid limply off the front of the boat.

With one gone, he was able to maneuver easier against the other two zombies. They were clinging to his legs and feet. As he kicked them away, he reached out against the bridge pilings, struggling to turn the boat into the current.

More zombies came spilling on top of them. Patrick was nearly knocked overboard by a falling body. As he lay stretched out, clinging to one of the swivel chairs to prevent himself from spilling over the side, one of them grabbed at his ankle. Hands were drawing his ankle to the zombie's waiting, snapping jaws. Another pair of hands grabbed at his ankle. There were two piling on top of him.

Patrick turned in surprise as he was suddenly released from their grasp. He turned to see Justin, having just emerged from below-decks, with a knife in either hand. He had skewered both of the zombies' skulls onto the deck.

Justin yawned. He looked around sleepily. "I'm out of it for a while and all hell br—"

He was stopped short of finishing, as zombies fell across him. They had apparently rolled off from the fishing tower above the cabin. They didn't come feet first, nor at the same velocity.

"Happy to return the favor." Patrick grunted as he stabbed the two zombies that had fallen across Justin. They we're beginning to writhe feverishly atop the live meat. Patrick pulled the first body off of Justin and slumped it over the boat rails. He pulled up on the corpse's legs and the rest slid over the side.

There was finally a reprieve from the falling bodies, as the boat drifted under the bridge. Zombies had begun collecting at the base of the bridge pilings, like a seething undead reef. The water under the bridge was a thick stew of zombies. They could hear them scraping and banging against the keel of the boat, as it slipped past them.

After a couple moments of shelter under the bridge, they had mostly removed the threat. They watched as the far side of the bridge began to drip with zombies as the hoards above shifted towards them.

"Get ready for round two!" Isherwood called out. "Look, we've got no anchor anymore and they're still coming. Padre, let's use the grappling hook on the pipeline to hold the boat in place."

"Or just motor to shore," Justin said, sliding into the captain's seat and revving up the inboard motors.

"Won't they start collecting against the boat if we anchored or whatever down from the bridge?" Patrick asked.

"Yeah, maybe," Isherwood answered. They were having to yell to be heard. The moans of the dead were echoing loudly in the cavern made between the water and the underside of the bridge. "But they won't be able to climb on board regardless, and they'll eventually slough off back into the current."

"Let's give it a try," Padre nodded. "The zees are still too thick coming off that bridge and everywhere else to attempt a landing. Besides, if we can keep drawing them into the water, we might be able to clean out this whole area, or at least the island. We could use the island, I think."

"Fine," Justin relented. "Try that hook-gun thing. If it doesn't work, I'll have the boat ready to drive us ashore."

"I thought of something else to get me on that pipe—" Isherwood began, but wasn't able to finish.

"Heads up!" Patrick called out as more zombies began thudding against the boat. They were passing now under the other side of the bridge. The echo chamber of moans dissipated as they floated past the bridge.

Fewer zombies were dragging their broken legs across the bridge deck this time. And there was no element of surprise this go-around. The men quickly dispatched the zombies with their knives and Isherwood's katana.

"Shoot, man." Patrick howled in surprise. He was clutching his ear after Isherwood's blade had passed inches from his head. "Be careful with that thing, or you'll Van Gogh me." They would find out later that, though the injury had been surprising bloodless, the sword had actually sliced into Patrick's ear a half-inch or so.

"Oh, dang. I'm so sorry." Isherwood raised his hands in apology.

"I'm okay," Patrick waved him off. "Just help me with this massive hairy beast, eh?" Isherwood had stabbed his sword through the temple of an unusually large zombie.

"Good Lord," Isherwood breathed in deeply. "Where'd this Gump come from? Justin, can you give us a hand?"

Justin ignored them. He was busy steering the boat into the current and keeping it away from the shore. There was some minor turbulence downstream of the bridge. Padre, however, had finished disposing of the zombies on the forward deck and was climbing to the back. As he passed, he checked out the fishing tower above the cabin. He was greeted with a gruesome sight.

Apparently, a zombie had fallen across the tower railing at just the right angle. It had been a youngish man, maybe college age. He was, incredibly, still wearing his college hat. One of his legs was resting on the fishing tower and sort of scratching back and forth. The other leg was swinging over the other side of the railing. The railing, itself, was lodged somewhere inside his chest cavity. The round metal rail had split him up the middle. If it wasn't for the creature's sternum and rib cage, the railing would have perfectly bisected him.

Isherwood followed Padre's eyes to the fishing tower. He winced, "How the heck? Didn't that dude have a hip bone or something?"

"Ouch!" Patrick said, finally noticing the grizzly sight. "That's just not supposed to happen."

Padre just shook his head. He unsheathed one of the rifles from his across his back. In one whirling motion, he slammed the thing across the neck and face. Slowly at first, the split zombie began tilting over the side. By the time Padre had slipped into the back of the boat, the thing had fallen off the boat and splashed into the water.

*****

"Okay, you got it in your sights, Padre?" Justin called up to the priest, who was standing on the fishing platform above the cabin area. He was aiming an AR rifle at the pipeline.

Justin was trying to keep the boat steady. He had turned the boat downstream, but had thrown the inboard motors in reverse slowing their progress downstream. He thought it would be smoother than pointing the boat upstream against the current.

Isherwood had snuck in one last idea to his scheme of anchoring off the pipeline. If they purposefully overshot the pipeline with the grappling hook, he thought, he could retrieve the hook end, tie onto it, and ride it up to the pipeline as the boat pulled the line downstream. This way he wouldn't have to climb up – he'd just ride up.

The grappling hook, an Army-issue launched grappling hook or LGH, was made to attach to the end of an AR rifle and was launched with a bullet catch. They

S. L. Smith

had tied the grappling hook, itself, onto the remaining anchor line. They didn't want to successfully launch over the pipeline only to have the whole thing get torn from the boat accidentally. They had pulled out the remaining line from the anchor mount, hoping it would uncoil smoothly when the hook was launched. The line that came with the LGH felt pretty thin, anyway. It probably was just enough for a man to climb on, but not enough to hold a large boat against the current. At least, that was what they decided after a quick fifteen second discussion.

"Ready," Padre called back from above.

Isherwood was starting to feel the blood drain from his head as he stared up at the pipeline. It was a good thirty feet above the water. He had thought it could work, but he hadn't – until just now – started visualizing himself making the climb. But then, he thought about how his father-in-law had sounded over the radio. Weak. Really weak. He'd never heard the man's voice sound like that. He also began to think about his wife, too. He couldn't let Sara down. He couldn't let his kids down. "What the hell am I doing?" He couldn't help but mumble to himself.

"Having cold feet, buddy?" Patrick asked. He was standing beside Isherwood in the back of the boat, which was now facing upstream and towards the pipeline and bridge.

"More like *wet* feet." Isherwood said, shaking his head. "Wet pants, too. I think I might have already wet myself."

"You'll be okay." Patrick reassured him.

"How do you know?"

"Because you have to be."

"Okay." Isherwood nodded in satisfaction. "That actually makes me feel better. Thanks." He tapped his pocket and necklace a few more times to make sure his rosary and rings were safe. He always strung his rings through his necklace when getting into dicey situations, which was pretty much constantly these days. He clicked into place the chest straps of the backpack he was wearing. It was filled with provisions for the starving family and was pretty heavy. It also had a shortwave radio in it, so he could communicate with the boat once he was ready for pickup.

He looked ridiculous trying to put on a backpack while still wearing the two swords strapped across his back.

"Whoa," Justin said glancing back toward Isherwood. "We're doing this *now*?"

"No time like the present," Isherwood answered.

Instead of protesting, Justin started giggling like a school girl. "I'm sorry – oh my God, I'm sorry."

"What?" Isherwood was smiling despite himself and his predicament.

"It's just. Oh, sweet –" Just squealed obnoxiously. "With the backpack and the swords! Tur—tur—you look just like a ninja tur—tur—TURTLE!" He mumbled something else resembling "kowabunga" and then dissolved into laughter.

Padre eventually interrupted Justin's giggle fit by firing the AR and launching the hook. Their heads all jerked skyward. The anchor line uncoiled smoothly from the front deck as the hook shot high above the air. Patrick whooped as the hook cleared the pipeline.

The line suddenly tightened and snapped taut. The hook seemed to hover for a second in the air. Then, the line relaxed as the hook came plummeting down on the upstream side of the pipeline. It splashed into the water ahead of them. For a moment, the anchor line seemed to form a perfect triangle rising up from the anchor mount and sloping back down into the water.

"Alright, turtle power," Justin said wiping away tears of laughter, as the submerged hook began floating towards the boat. "It's all you." He may have mumbled some words of concern between further giggles, but no one could really tell.

Isherwood didn't hear anything further from Justin. All he could hear was the blood pounding in his head as his ladder skyward drew nearer. Isherwood dropped down into a crouch on the boat deck. It helped him conceal the sudden weakness he felt in his knees.

"Here," Padre said after climbing down from the tower and stowing away the rifle. "Take these. For the rope." He tossed a pair of gloves towards Isherwood. He thought that the priest might have sensed that his hands were sweating, or maybe just saw the wet smears across the deck.

By the time he had put on the gloves, the rope was nearly to the boat. It was passing close to the boat but still out of arm's reach. Patrick grabbed a fishing pole that he'd found on the boat. He leaned over the boat's starboard side and snagged the anchor line on the first try. As Patrick pulled the line in, the hook remained submerged.

Padre grabbed a hold of the line and quickly tied a loop into it. "Here," he said, holding the loop near the deck. "Isherwood, put your foot put in here. Quick. This'll make the ascent easier. Just don't get your foot permanently caught in it, okay?"

"Thanks, Padre." He said, stepping into the loop and grabbing a hold of the line, as well. The line was slowly rising back up to the pipeline as the boat crept downstream. The plan was to turn the boat back into the current and reverse the engines once Isherwood was clear and up on the pipeline. They wanted the anchor mount facing the pipeline once the line was secured to it.

It wasn't long before Isherwood felt the tug of the rising line. As he was lifted in the air, they looked up to the pipeline, listening for any signs of distress. The pipeline didn't even wobble.

"Whoa, man." Justin said shielding his eyes as he looked up. "This might actually work."

CHAPTER FIVE:

RINGLING BROTHERS

It did work. Isherwood didn't exactly climb onto the pipeline. He was dragged over the top of it. He just barely got his foot free of the rope loop before being yanked down into the infested river.

Isherwood just lay there clinging to the topside of the wide pipeline. Justin and the boys were giving him thumbs-up from the boat deck below. *Far* below, it seemed. The boat was about a mile below him, Isherwood estimated. His eyes swam. He choked down the contents of his belly as his stomach lurched. Acid burned through his sinuses.

Despite the burning liquid dripping from his nose, he was able to secure the anchor line to the pipeline. With the remaining slack in the line, he was able to swing the hook under the pipeline so that it came swinging upward on the down-stream side. The hook nearly embedded itself in Isherwood's eye socket. He caught it, tucked it under the anchor line, and knotted it. Somehow, he appeared – at least to the guys down on the boat below – to seem pretty adept at what he was doing. He wouldn't be able to remember any of this later.

Somehow, he managed to turn himself around and shimmy a couple hundred yards down the pipe. Again, he would later be unable to recall getting across the pipeline. He would say the angels carried him. As it was, he saw they were wise not to wait for the shoreline to clear. Zombies must be spilling over the bridge onto the land, as well as the water, he thought. He could see that what they were doing was working, really working. He just hoped that the pipeline took him past the throngs pressing against the sides of the pilot channel. Even if the pipeline could take him into the clear, if they spotted him, he knew they would swarm the base of it before he could get clear. He thought for sure they had seen him climb onto the pipeline.

The pipeline curved sharply back into the ground on its far western end. As he approached the sharp turn, Isherwood saw green grass and smiled. Seeing the grass, he knew he hadn't been swarmed. But it was tall grass. Tall grass is scary grass, Isherwood thought. As he slid down the pipeline, slowed by the junction collars, he saw that he had not been spared a welcome party, after all.

He hit the ground hard, cursing under his breath. The gentle curve of the pipe straightened suddenly, and he basically fell the last ten feet or so. Luckily, the ground was soft and damp. His boots nearly disappeared into sludge. He toppled over and landed on all fours. His hands were gloved with mud, but at least, he thought, his side arms hadn't fallen into the mud.

With a loud slurping sound, he pulled his boots free of the mud. Arms lurched after him from the far side of the pipeline, but the mud slowed the already slow zombies.

He darted away from the end of the pipeline as fast as he could. He kept his feet moving to avoid sinking into the mud, even walking on all fours. Staying mobile, he knew, was the best way to avoid getting surrounded. This place had to be littered with oncoming zombies staggering towards the channel.

He looked ahead down a long clear line cut through the otherwise thick forest and undergrowth. They called it a "cut" or "cut-through," maybe because it looked like a razor had just cut a bald streak through a thick head of hair. There were deer stands set up at intervals along the length of the pipeline cut-through. These, Isherwood knew, would be a tempting place to hide in if he got caught in a tight spot. However, the ten, twenty, and sometimes thirty-foot plywood boxes on stilts would quickly become death traps if swarmed. They would be top-heavy, too. No, he thought, it would serve only as a measure of last resort.

As he jogged down the pipeline, he could see heads and slumping torsos rising here and there from the tall grass. "Come out to the coast, we'll get together, have a few laughs," he mumbled to himself as he dodged here and there through puddles and pockets of mud.

Though he would prefer to have a sword in either hand, he was keeping his hands free, if only because he kept stumbling onto all fours. He needed to re-member the lessons he learned in Kindergarten about running with scissors, much less samurai swords. If he wasn't careful, he might accidentally perform suppuku on himself, falling bowels-first onto the blade.

Isherwood had been mentally planning his route inland to his in-laws camp. He had been forcing himself to think about it, actually. It was better than ruminating on the dizzying heights of the pipeline or the feeling of being watched by a thousand eyes.

He had a good mental map of the island in his head. He was looking over it as he jogged along one side of the cut-through. He needed to go about half a mile or so west along the cut-through. He would be paralleling the path of the I-10 overpass about another half mile north. After that half mile, he would run across another, slightly narrower cut through. This second cut would lead diagonally south and further west to the camp. If he needed to, he could leave the cut. The going would be much slower, though, through the undergrowth.

******

Isherwood was making steady progress down the cut-through. He was now less than a hundred yards from the intersection of the pipeline cut and the cut that would lead to the camp. In hindsight, he should have approached the intersection with greater caution. He had just assumed that the numbers of the dead would diminish the farther he moved inland. They didn't.

Isherwood was nearly face to face with a dozen zombies before he realized his mistake. A group of zombies had coalesced just south of the intersection. In the back of Isherwood's mind, he thought that maybe a raccoon or deer had been brought down by the zombies near here. The animal's screams had probably attracted a swarm. It could have been days ago, but the swarm had, apparently, not found a cause to move on from the spot. Until now.

Thinking quickly – he had already mused about a strategy for a situation like this – Isherwood darted north through the intersection. He was moving in the opposite direction from the camp. *Just as well*, he thought to himself, breathing deeply to help regulate his heart rate. He had acquired a fair-size swarm of groupies following behind him, as well. He was headed straight for the woods on the north side of the intersection. He was clapping his hands as he went, too. He was going to lead them all, both swarms, into the woods and double-back. If he just dodged them now, he'd have to face them all over again when he had his in-laws in tow. He would likely be moving much slower by that point, and the double-back maneuver would not be impossible. He actually anticipated doing a few of these clean-up maneuvers along the way – just in case he didn't find a suitable transport vehicle at the camp.

Leading north from the intersection, Isherwood was relieved to stumble across a trail. It was maybe five or six feet wide. It had been made for four-wheelers or Mules to drive through. It led, he thought, to a tree stand he had hunted the year before. If he remembered correctly, this path took him closer to the bayou. This meant *more* mud and likely large patches of standing water. His mind drifted to images of zombie mouths rising from the muddy water and snapping at him. He shook his head free of these images. He just hoped his rubber boots were bite-proof.

Once he had walked a few paces down the trail, he looked back to see what was following him. Even without turning, he could hear the clacking of teeth of the half dozen or so that were nearest him. The moans of these were rising nearly to shrieks. They sounded as though they could almost taste him. The nearest zombie was a squat black man with torn jeans. One entire pant leg was missing and he had worn the pads of his feet down to the bone. Isherwood labelled this one Derrick Todd Lee, the serial killer who had dumped his bodies under the I-10 bridge not far from this spot. Isherwood looked quickly away from the next zombie. It was a college-aged guy who looked every bit the part of a frat boy. Its collar was even still popped and sunglasses hung from a cord around its neck. From the waist down, however, he was naked. Isherwood winced as he looked away because there was only a dark hole where the frat boy's manhood was supposed to be. *Perhaps the Apocalypse reveals the truth, after all,* Isherwood thought to himself.

Isherwood could see that his plan was working. It was working a little too well, he thought. Behind the nearest group of dead stalking after him, behind Derrick and the frat boy, were nearly a hundred zombies. They were moving quickly, too. There was a sound of desperation in their moans, as though they hadn't seen live prey in a very long time.

The mobs of zombies disappeared as Isherwood turned a corner along the trail. He took the opportunity to dispatch the nearest zombies. There was an electric hum as he unsheathed the first katana. The frat boy and Derrick Todd were side by side now. Several more were also coming into view. Isherwood smirked. He reared back, intending to sweep off both their heads with one swing. The sword swept through the air. Unfortunately, he didn't take into account the difference in their heights. The sword lodged midway through Derrick's skull. It was enough to drop the black man, but frat-tastic was on Isherwood before he could get his second sword out.

Isherwood fell backward into the mud. He had been attacked while still off balance. He gave up on the sword and went for one of the 9mm pistols holstered at his sides. He pushed fratty's head back with his right hand against its forehead and the butt of the pistol under its chin. He fired. Still pinned under fratty, he aimed and fired at the remaining zombies still advancing on him. "I need to make noise, don't I?" He said out loud. "Then let's do it."

He scrambled out from under the frat boy and tried not to think about the stain its body had left behind. He put a boot against the base of Derrick's skull and slid the katana out with some difficulty. Looking up, he saw the main body of the hoard squeezing into the narrow trail. "That's right! Look at me. Come on, worm sacks. Focus on this guy."

After mocking the zombies a few seconds longer, he turned and ran. He needed to get out from the locus of the gunshots quickly. He ran about a quarter mile along the trail in a west-northwesterly direction. He fired a couple more shots towards the hoard which was now long out of sight. He wished he had a wind-up toy or an alarm clock to leave behind. He would need to add an item like that to his arsenal – just a cheap casio watch could do the trick, *if* he could program it in a pinch.

He left the trail and darted through the woods. He thought he had maybe a minute before his crashing through the woods would lead them off the trail. For now, he didn't think they were bright enough to sense the change in direction. He

S. L. Smith

hoped. In a minute, he bet that he could be back in the pipeline cut-through *and*, if he was quiet, out of dead ear shot. Regardless, he'd be putting some distance between himself and the hoard.

Whether for better or worse, he didn't know, but the undergrowth was pretty light getting back to the cut. The ground was full of palmettos, but he could mostly weave around these. He just hoped the piles of leaves didn't hide one of the deep holes left behind from a rotting cypress. Despite jumping over fallen logs and crashing through brambles without knowing what lay on the other side, he made it with both ankles intact.

It probably took him closer to five minutes to reach the cut, but he didn't care. He just wanted to be gone before the hoard started drifting out of the woods like a line of Confederate soldiers, as they had back at the levee in St. Maryville.

When he had finally returned to the intersection of the pipeline cut and the cut which would lead him to his in-law's camp, he paused panting. He ducked behind a tree while he briefly scanned the intersection and caught his breath. It had worked! The place was deserted. He could hear, not see, maybe one or two stragglers, but it had worked. Without waiting for his pulse to settle down, he pushed himself onward. He didn't want to screw up a job well done. Plus, he was nearly there. He could almost taste the sweetness of the rescue.

CHAPTER SIX: THE CAMP

Isherwood saw or heard only scattered zombies as he speed-walked a mile or so down the second cut. The adrenaline of the double-back maneuver gradually gave way once more to the exhilaration of the rescue mission. Nevertheless, he began ticking off a list of possible scenarios he might encounter at the camp. Disregarding injuries and half-starved relatives, he may well be walking into a massive swarm still surrounding the camp. He had begun to doubt this possibility, though. He was now close enough to the camp to hear the tell-tale signs of a swarm, especially in a swamp, if the dead had amassed in such numbers. There would be a smothering roar of moans. There would also be the insectile clicking of a thousand feet slapping and mounding in the mud. There would also be an overpowering stench of death, like opening a casket.

Isherwood guessed that there were just enough zombies still gathering around the camp to keep his family pinned in. Most had probably drifted towards the ruckus in the Pilot Channel, and his father-in-law, Glenn, was too smart to draw them right back in with gunfire. They had likely heard the pop-pop of his pistol, as well, and knew that Isherwood was on his way.

This was what he was hoping, anyway, as he came around the last turn. He had slowed his approach significantly. The sound of his footsteps were now barely audible, though the pounding in his chest seemed to him almost deafening. Around the far side of the next tree, he thought he'd finally be able to see the camp.

There it was. In a dark hollow of trees, a wood-shingled box rose above the swamp on narrow legs. There were no architectural adornments to the simple structure, but it was sizeable. It could sleep nearly twenty people in bunk beds. If not for the misfortune of the swarm and proximity to I-10, it would have served as a great hideout. And may yet.

Though he could see the structure, Isherwood could not yet see what, if anything, was assailing it. There was a rise in the land between him and the camp. It blocked his line of sight to the camp's footings. Isherwood momentarily considered shooting his pistol into the air to draw what zombies were in the area to him and performing another double-back maneuver. He shook off the thought. This could very likely do more harm than good. The camp might actually be swarm-free. He scoffed at himself for thinking the world of zombies might cut him a break. He survived by banking on Murphy's Law, not ignoring it.

There was a roofed structure between him and the rise before the camp. It was an open-air tractor barn, like a carport for heavy equipment. He ducked down and sprinted over to it. There were plenty of places to take cover between the rusting hulks. He leaned back against a stacked pile of fifty-pound bags of deer corn and rice bran. He sniffed at them absent-mindedly. They didn't smell of rot and may prove useful in the short-term. He listened for a moment for the clumsy sounds of approaching zombies. He was clear.

He again inched around his cover and spied the path ahead. There was an overgrown stand of crape myrtles that had been planted to sell. They stood off to his side. These were too thick and offered little room to maneuver. He would need to mount the small hill before the camp. He would be in the open for the 180 degrees at his back, he thought. He would still be hidden, however, from what lay beyond if he stayed just below the hill's crest.

He was soon slicing through the tall grass in a crouched run, without giving his plan a second thought. As he crouched below the crest of the hill, his head spun back and forth along the dirt road which cleaved into the hill. It was already too late, there was at least one zombie in either direction. They spotted his darting movements immediately. Isherwood could sense, rather than hear, the gurgling air bubbles rising up their dead, occluded lungs. Soon, twin moans had shattered the stillness, like the cries of buglers. The battle for the camp has begun.

Both zombies were still far off, though he thought he could hear something stirring in the grass behind and closer to him. He ignored all these threats for the moment. He slowly raised his head over the crest of the hill to finally see what lay at the camp's feet.

"That's it?" Isherwood said aloud, suddenly. He stood up and walked straight toward the camp. There were only six or seven zombies. He again spoke aloud, "Either they're in worse shape than I thought, or I'm already too late."

Unsheathing the first katana, he leaped towards the first zombie just as it was turning to greet him. Bringing the full momentum of his body to bear, the thing's came tumbling down. The next wide sweep of the blade was much clumsier. The sword sank deep into one of the timber pilings supporting the camp overhead. "Crap!" Isherwood cursed at himself. "I've got to get better at this!"

Unsheathing his backup katana, he circled around the camp's underside in a slowly narrowing spiral. At the center of his spiral, lay the foot of the stairs leading up to the camp. This, too, he soon realized was filled with a line of waiting zombies. "Okay, alright, that's probably enough to trap them." If he moved efficiently, he thought, he could make this into the Battle of Sterling Bridge, where William Wallace and the Scots mowed down the English has they slowly crossed the narrow passage. His object would be to prevent their swarming. If he was quick, he could mow them down one-by-one as they came tumbling down the stairs. *Maybe.* He thought.

He finished cleaning up around the base of the stairs and had completed his circuit just as the zombies we're beginning to spill down the stairs. The ascending line of rotting flesh was soon spilling over itself in a bloody frenzy. Their clumsiness served them well. As they tumbled down onto one another in a messy, bile-strewn heap, Isherwood's strategy was defeated.

He had mowed down all the standing and staggering zombies. He was now hacking away at the things that came crawling towards him. They were spilling out from a mound forming at the base of the stairs. Wet with filth, they almost slithered out of the pile like a tangled brood of vipers. "Fantastic," Isherwood said as he spat out nastiness that had sprayed into his open mouth. "I'm gonna hafta walk through all this mess."

He wiped the sweat and gore from his face, as a fine red-black mist began rising in the air, It had been fanned upward by the rapidly swirling and slashing katana blade. "Screw it." He said, sheathing his blade. He leapt up and grabbed one of the wooden stair steps. He tried pulling himself up and onto the landing. It would have been a short cut, but his hands slipped on something soft and revolting on the step above. He just managed to land on his feet as he came tumbling back down. Humbled, he moved back to his spot at the foot of the stairs and resumed hacking away.

The two zombies that had spotted him as he hid against the crest of the hill were slowly staggering towards the camp. He remembered to keep an eye out for these. Sure enough, another three zombies came stumbling towards him from behind. He was a very inhospitable host to the oncoming neighbors. He turned and sliced off their heads one at a time. The blade felt like it was growing warm within his grasp. It was either that, Isherwood thought, or the heads were just cleaving off easier.

Though it felt both longer and shorter, it took Isherwood another five minutes to clear the steps. He had been forced to stomp across a number of skulls and sick, rotting faces. This was the way he held their quivering heads still as he lobbed off the heads. He was reminded of the Queen of Hearts as he worked through the crowd. "I feel like Henry or Queen Elizabeth massacring the Catholics," he joked aloud breathlessly.

Finally, he stood halfway up the steps. He was panting as though he'd been swinging an axe the whole time. The katana was much lighter than an axe or most any other swinging weapon, but even it took his toll. Sweat and gore was dripping from his face. His white eyes shined from the dark muck coating his face as though he had anointed his face with shoe polish.

"You just gonna stand there?" A voice called from above. The stairs led up to something of a trap door in the camp floor above. The originally stairway, leading to the camp's front porch, had been hastily destroyed. The stairway leading up to the trapdoor had been allowed to remain, because, even with the stairs, the trap door was only reachable when a ladder was lowered onto the stair's topmost landing. It was perfect for the occupants' current predicament.

Isherwood tilted half of his face upward, too tired to lift his whole head. He smiled wryly at the face he saw there. It was a thinned face, which had grown rapidly careworn since he had seen it last. It was his father-in-law, Glenn.

"Didn't you use to have some color in that beard?" Isherwood asked the older man. Glenn moved his hand as though to rub his chin whiskers, but stopped short.

Glenn's eyes re-focused on something behind Isherwood. He nodded down the stairs. Isherwood had begun turning as soon as Glenn's eyes had twitched. As he turned, he drew the katana upward into a defensive position. One twitch of Isherwood's arm while holding the sword at this angle, and he could dispatch a zombie.

The creature was still several feet down. It was clinging to the side railing for support, because its foot had been lobbed off. This had probably occurred while Isherwood was slicing and dicing the huddle of fallen zombies. Isherwood shuffled down a few steps and quickly tidied up the matter. He had the high ground, after all. The blade sliced neatly between two of the creature's cervical vertebrae. The head slapped down against the blood-tinted mud below and the body, slumping over the railing, soon followed.

During the body's inexorable slide off the railing, Isherwood took a moment to check out the area surrounding the camp. There were a few zombies beginning to appear around the perimeter. He turned back to see Glenn nodding appreciatively at his handiwork. Isherwood was surprised at how gratifying it was to receive this unspoken praise. He had always admired his father-in-law's skills as a sportsman. That is, as a hunter and tracker. Isherwood had caught on quickly, but he never felt he would have the skills of someone who grew up around this stuff. His household's only rifle before all this zombie mess actually belonged to his wife. But he realized suddenly that he might have more natural ability that he ever imagined.

Isherwood pushed all these thoughts aside, returning to the present. "Where's the nearest vehicle?" He asked, rapidly switching gears. "How many survivors, Glenn?"

Glenn was prepared for both of these questions. Isherwood, however, was unprepared for the sight of Glenn. He pulled himself up and through the trap door.

His father-in-law was severely emaciated, though his eyes, thankfully, had lost none of their sharpness.

"Jesse's camp," Dale answered, regarding the nearest vehicle. Isherwood wanted to ask how that could've happened. They always had a mule or four-wheeler or truck on hand. But he had prepared himself for this answer when he didn't see any vehicles when he first approached the camp.

"What is it? Keys in the ignition?" Isherwood asked hurriedly, but was soon distracted. There were no foul smells coming from inside the camp, aside from the mustiness of people living for extended periods without showering. This was itself a good sign. That means that no one had died, likely – though the dead these days had a habit of walking off – and they had strength enough to dispose of their excrement, likely out of a window.

Isherwood was distracted by the faces of his wife's family staring back at him. Their eyes were large, but not because of the excitement at seeing Isherwood. It was because of their obvious state of malnutrition. They smiled up at him weakly.

Isherwood jerked suddenly, as though he'd been shocked by a live wire. "Food! Of course! I'm so sorry. I've been carrying this so long – I just forgot." He pulled off his swords and holsters and let it all clatter to the wood floor. He fumbled at his backpack, which Justin had not long ago compared to a turtle shell. He struggled to unhook the chest straps and barely noticed the relief in his shoulders as he slid the pack off.

Glenn was still sitting beside the trap door, having already exhausted himself with just the opening of the door. The rest of the family, at least all of the women, were huddled together on a futon couch. Sara's two brothers were sitting on the floor along the walls. The center of the camp was an open floor plan of kitchen transitioning into den. The bunkrooms were beyond the central room on either side. Porches wrapped around the camp on two sides.

Isherwood was moving quickly now. He hurried over to the futon and began passing out water bottles. He had to unscrew the caps for them, because even that, despite their obvious thirst, was overwhelming. He looked into his pack at all the PowerBars he had brought along, and realized that they'd never be able to chew let alone swallow them.

The whole family was temporarily dazed, ecstatically gulping down the water. They didn't even notice the look of thought and confusion on Isherwood's face. He dug down deeper into the pack, and found some chocolate bars. "Here," he said, unwrapping and distributing the mix of Hershey and Godiva. "This'll give you a quick jolt of energy. Because you're gonna need it. Really need it."

He retreated to the kitchen area. "There, eat that," he was saying, mostly to himself. "And I'll figure out these PowerBars." They weren't exactly PowerBars, or he would've been in for a serious hassle. They were some sort of dense granola bar. He grabbed some plastic bowls and spoons, which were depressingly unused, and began grinding up the bars into crumbs. Soon, he had something resembling a cereal. He poured water into it, stirred, and made sort of a mash. He darted around giving out the bowls.

"There," he said, as they all started to eat with renewed vigor. "Let's see," Isherwood said counting off with his fingers and trying to lighten the mood. "Feed the hungry. Give drink to the thirsty. Heal the sick. Visit the imprisoned. Bury the dead, or at least hack off their heads. That's like five corporal works of mercy."

"You're almost as good as a mother." Missy, his mother-in-law, whispered softly. Isherwood laughed, and the others attempted smiles.

"Alrighty." Isherwood said heavily, bringing his mind back around to their predicament. "Okay. Y'all eat that up as fast as you can, but not too fast. Get some energy back into your bones. I'll go see what I can do about that – what'd you say it was? – at Jesse's."

"It's a truck." Glenn said, speaking with a full mouth of food. "Keys in the visor, hopefully. Don't think he ever touched 'em." Glenn finished ominously.

Isherwood nodded, understanding all too well what Glenn would only hint at. "Here's my pack. I'll leave it right here. There's more provision inside, plus some spare weapons. Be ready to leave in about five minutes. If I'm not back in five minutes, I'm hotwiring."

"Hotwiring?" Glenn raised an eyebrow appreciatively.

"Yeah," Isherwood smiled proudly. "I can do that now. You're brother-in-law taught me."

Isherwood put his arms back through the double sword sheath and adjusted the straps across his chest. He was still down to one sword, as the other was still cleaved into one of the camp's support pilings. He also returned the double holster to his hips. "I'll leave you with one of these, though." He said, placing a fully loaded 9mm on the kitchen counter. Seconds later, he was gone.

CHAPTER SEVEN:

BARNSTOKK

Isherwood dropped silently through the trap door and onto the stairs below. There was a welcoming party, but he was relieved there weren't more. "Y'all are like rats, you know?" He whispered, as he skullcapped a nicely dressed woman, likely another interstate zombie. "Or girl scouts. Turn your back for just a second, and you've come spilling out of the woodwork."

He wanted to heave himself onto the railing of the stairway and swing his feet into the chest of the next oncoming zombie, but he held himself back. It was easier to chop them down, one by one, as he descended the stairs. Besides, he thought, the railings were slick with gore and nastiness. Just his luck, he goes sliding down into the hacked up dogpile he had created earlier.

He struggled to retrieve his sword from the wood piling. It was easy to overestimate the sharpness and power of this sword, Isherwood thought as he saw how far the blade had sank into the wood. He didn't have the time to do this correctly, even if he knew how. He stabbed one sword into the soft earth. Looking around, he kicked his foot up onto the timber post. He then jumped up and grabbed the hilt of the sword and then let the weight of his fall jerk down on the sword. He did this a few more times. It hadn't budged.

"Oh, come on!" Isherwood called out, a little too loud. He was suddenly aware of the pain and fatigue in his arms and legs, and of the cold sweat at the back of his neck that meant heat exhaustion.

"Alright, have it your way. Give me my sword," and he pulled again at the sword. The sword came out smoothly this time, as if it lay loose for him. "Whoa." He coughed, looking down suspiciously at the sword in his hand. He quickly looked around. He shook his head, disappointed that no one had seen it. Not even a zombie. He reached up along the timber piling, just above where the sword had been embedded only a moment ago. He felt something written there. There were letters carved into the wood.

"Probably Croatoan." He said, rolling his eyes. He pulled up on the wood to get a better look. "Barstool? Must be a manufacturer's mark or something stupid. No, wait. It's Barnstokk? What the heck is that?" He shook his head, assuming it was some Norwegian timber producer or something, and walked off toward the next camp.

****

Sunlight glinting off green paint caught Isherwood's eye. Jesse's camp lay at the end of the dirt road Isherwood had crossed over when he first came into the camp. A green trunk sat in front of it. Isherwood could feel, rather than see, shadows moving between the pilings of Jesse's camp. He didn't want to encounter the dead version of Jesse. Hopefully, he was thinking to himself, the keys would be exactly where Glenn had said. Under the visor.

The truck was a small Isuzu or Mitsubishi affair. "A golf cart?" Isherwood whispered to himself. "I'm supposed to rescue a family the size of a small village with *this*? Might as well take the slather-ourselves-with-rotting-guts approach."

He lifted the door handle. The thing squealed back at him, like a frightened chicken. A second later, the noise was answered by several moans from under Jesse's camp. "Fantastic." Isherwood moaned. He thought to himself, *at least it was unlocked*. He slid into the small cab of the truck, resting his swords in the passenger seat, and closed the door behind him. The door howled in protest as he did. *Only seconds now*, he thought. "If the keys aren't up –"

Isherwood suddenly dove into the passenger side of the truck. The gear sheet rammed up into his gut. "Cuss-biscuits!" He howled in pain before opening his eyes and realizing that he had come a hair's breadth from slicing off his face on the sword. He looked back towards the window, expecting to see a zombie about to spill into the already-tight cab with him. There was just a blood smear of a hand. Soon, a dark, mouldering face careened into sight. It was pressing itself slowly against the window.

"Let's try this again," Isherwood said, as more bodies began hurling themselves at the little truck. Despite the panic rising in his chest, he took a second to say a prayer that the keys were about to spill into his lap.

"Sweet baby Jesus!" He squealed when the keys full into his lap. "Let's do this," he said suddenly feeling optimistic. The engine turned over after only a couple tries. "Alright," he said, and pushed down slowly on the accelerator.

Nothing. He could hear the whine of the rear wheel drive, but the vehicle wasn't budging. He looked into the rear-view mirror, and saw something awful. He could see the shape of a man through the muck-encrusted window. It was Jesse. Or was. It had been Sara's favorite uncle, he thought to himself. And now, he was a giant speed bump.

The truck was really not much more than a compact car in size. Isherwood could have likely picked up the front half bare-handed. There was little to no heft to the vehicle. Even if he wanted to, he couldn't nudge the Jesse-zombie out of the way. Plowing right over him was out of the question. He felt like he was backing into a tree, or at least a stump. He could go forward, though, thankfully.

He took a few seconds to roll down the windows a half inch or so. It was wide enough for the blade of a sword but not the hilt. He knocked a couple quick holes into the heads of the zombies at his flanks, and pulled forward. He would make a loop around the back of the camp, and hopefully lose the walking remains of his wife's uncle in the process. This was a zombie kill he was desperately hoping to avoid. At the same time, he didn't want the others to see him. Their morale was a precious quantity.

He decided that he couldn't risk the LaGranges seeing Jesse. He waited until the bear-size zombie staggered around the camp into his rear-view mirror. He kicked the driver's door open. The door howled in protest. "I know, I know," Isherwood answered the door. "I don't want to do it. I have to."

He turned to face the Goliath zombie. "Why do y'all have to look so much like your former selves? But still so completely changed?" He aimed the katana's swing into the thickness of the man's mossy beard.

"Again?" Isherwood seethed with anger. The katana had lodged itself again. The man's spinal column was apparently unnaturally thick. Isherwood stepped back quickly to dodge the man's heavy paw as it bore down on him. He ran back to the green truck and grabbed the second sword from the passenger seat. "That's twice now that I'd've been sunk without a backup." Isherwood said, disregarding the pistol.

Isherwood returned with the second katana and pivoted around the massive zombie. He brought the blade down against the back of the man's neck as he did. From this angle, the zombie looked almost as he had in life. He brushed away the sudden rush of memories to finish the job.

He retrieved his sword and did a quick scan of the area. He was alone for the moment. There was a ring of logs around a long-spent bonfire. He dragged Jesse's body into the fire ring and tipped the ash pile onto the body. He finished covering Jesse as best he could with handfuls of ash. He crossed the dead man's forehead and turned back to the truck.

Moments later, he was rolling over the hill back to the LaGrange camp. His thoughts had turned to the bed of the truck. He was worried it would be too small to hold everybody. Even if it did, except for inside the cab, there was no room to retreat from the reaching, grabbing hands of the dead. The women would have to ride inside the cab with him, while Glenn and his sons rode in the bed. It could work, he thought, but they would need a hefty measure of luck. So much depended on how quickly the boat could retrieve them from the beach. *And what depth of zombies they would be wading into.*

*****

When Isherwood returned through the trapdoor, the family was beginning to show signs of life. The children, at least, most of which were teenagers, were already recovering from the advanced stages of starvation. Isherwood guessed that Glenn and Missy had been sacrificing their own rations for the children, likely without the kids realizing it. He saw that they would need to carry Missy out of the camp. Glenn, Isherwood knew, would never permit anyone to carry him out of his own home. It was just as well, Isherwood's own head was starting to grow fuzzy from prolonged exposure and fighting.

Sarah's two brothers, Micha and Eli, helped Isherwood lower their mother through the opening in the floor and down the steps. Isherwood broke away from them to start sweeping the perimeter as the other started spilling through the trap door. Though their food supplies had been long depleted, Glenn and the boys were still well armed with sidearms, rifles, shotguns, and hunting bows. They had a duffel bag of their own packed and ready. They had also filled Isherwood's backpack, now emptied of provisions, with all the spare ammo it could hold. He grabbed the radio out of the bag before it was loaded.

Isherwood had parked the green truck near the foot of the stairs which led to the trap door. The foot of the steps was still clogged with the pile of minced zombies from Isherwood's arrival. Missy was able to help lift herself into the passenger seat of the truck and the girls, Mary and Annie, somehow piled in beside her.

Somehow, they had all fit into the cab and bed along with the bags of weapons and ammo by the time Isherwood returned. It took him a full five minutes to clear the area, though his back had been unburdened of his pack. He was growing tired and the zombies were growing more numerous.

"Okay," Isherwood said, returning out of breath. "This is a pretty good set up. Glenn in the center with the shotgun. Micah and Eli at the front and sides. Once we get away from this fixed location, the sound of gunfire won't be such a bad thing. It might even start drawing the zombies away from the edge of the Pilot Channel and give the guys in the boat a heads-up we're coming."

"They're lining the beaches?" Eli asked incredulously.

"Oh yeah," Isherwood answered with wide eyes. "For miles. They're just throwing themselves into the channel and getting swept away. It's clearing the whole area, but it must be all of Baton Rouge and Lafayette spilling off the Interstate."

"But why?" Micah asked, smirking. "Why're they doing that?"

"Why are the dead committing suicide?" Isherwood smirked back. Micah nodded. He seemed to shrink in confidence. "Because Padre and the others are sitting ducks in a boat in the middle of the channel, or at least they seem to be."

"Fishing with live bait?" Eli, the older brother, was nodding in approval. "Alright."

"Yeah," Isherwood said, feeling a sudden rush of anxiety. "For as long as we can." His eyes suddenly had a faraway look in them. He slammed the tailgate into place, and turned toward the cab.

"Get ready, guys. The mobs can get really thick, really fast." Isherwood saw their hands tighten subconsciously around the stocks and barrels of their shotguns. "Light it up. They'll know we're coming, either way."

"You killed a bunch of them," Annie remarked as Isherwood clanged the driver's door shut and got the engine going again. Annie and Mary were basically sitting on top of him. He had placed the radio in his lap for the drive. Annie leaned over and wiped a smudge of blood from his forehead. "You're covered in this stuff, Ish."

"We're still a long way from a hot shower, but it's — it's in sight. Almost. Let's get out of here, okay?" He said as he shifted into reverse and pulled out from under the camp.

CHAPTER EIGHT:

OMAHA BEACH

Isherwood decided to take a different way back than he had come. That way, along the pipeline, was likely filled with zombies by now. The mob he had left behind had hopefully drawn others to it as they moaned in frustration. He slid the back window of the truck open, so he could talk to Glenn and the boys. They knew the island like the back of their hands, and he was going to need their advice.

As he drove over the hill and back along the road, he asked Glenn for an alternative route that would, hopefully, put them a ways south of the pipeline but still in sight of the boat. He would rather not take this approach, obviously, but if the radio failed him he could also honk the truck's horn at the boat. Hopefully, the boat would arrive faster than the swarm. Hopefully. Ideally, though, they would not even need to wait for the boat.

"Hey Glenn, are there any boats still docked on the island?"

"What?" Glenn asked, still not able to yell. Mary relayed the message for Isherwood. He could hear Glenn's reply, though it was too soft for him to make it out.

"He said," Mary relayed. "That there wouldn't be anything except at the main dock."

"Okay, that's what I figured." Isherwood answered. "Tell him we'll take the road that goes past there. If it's heavily infested, we'll keep driving on past down that road that parallels the west bank of the channel. We'll drive it until we find a quiet place to wait for the boat."

Isherwood next picked up the radio from his lap. With one hand still on the steering wheel, he turned the knob on the radio. "This is Isherwood. I've got the family in tow. There are six of us total. *All alive*, over!" He ended the last part with a sudden rush of emotion, and he almost choked up. His two sisters-in-law noticed, though. Annie leaned in closer and wrapped her arm around his neck. Mary, too, reached her hand over and gave Isherwood's head a scratch.

He hadn't yet had time to process that they were all still alive. Sara still had one unaccounted-for sister, Maggie. She was living in Baton Rouge when the power grid collapsed and all electronic-based communication stopped. To have them all here with him and alive, Isherwood smiled, was an incredible feeling. *If I can only keep it this way a little longer*, he thought. But he knew that their greatest challenge may yet lay ahead of them.

The radio crackled in response. "We're all just wasting away here in Margaritaville. Over." It was Justin.

"Brother," Isherwood answered. "It's good to hear your voice."

"Naturally," Justin interrupted. "Over. Wait, was that a *Lost* reference?"

"What?"

"You know, with 'the Island' and all. Nevermind. Over."

"Anyway, can y'all see the boat dock? I forgot to point it out before, which was *really* stupid. There should be a stop sign sticking up out of the water, a break in the trees, and some timber mats going up a hill. Is there a boat tied up there? Over."

"Let me get the binoculars. Hold on. Over." Justin answered, and the radio fell quiet.

Isherwood had turned now back onto the last cut-through. He turned southward on it, but took a second to look back the way he had come. There was movement down the cut. Shadowy figures were standing still at about two hundred yards. He could feel, rather than see, their necks snap in their direction.

"Mary, tell the boys to hold their fire until we get a few hundred yards down the cut. There's a mob down that way. A mean one."

As Mary relayed the message, the radio chirped. "We found it." It was Padre's voice this time. "It's good to hear your voice, Isherwood. That was some real 007 action on that pipeline. No boats at the dock, but plenty of zombies. Over."

"Good to hear y'all haven't had any more complications, too, Padre. Is it possible to clear out the area? Over." Isherwood asked.

After a long pause, Padre's voice returned. "It's hard to say. It may just draw more, while creating a barrier of bodies. Plus, we may need the ammo. Over."

"I gotcha." Isherwood answered. "Looks like we're gonna need the ramp, though. We've got some here with mobility issues. Over."

"Okay, we'll see what we can do. We're gonna detach from the pipeline and head closer to the west bank. We may be able to draw them away from the dock a bit before you get there. Over."

"I like it. Thank you. Over and out."

Isherwood put the radio down quickly. Not only was the truck getting together around potholes, they were beginning to encounter zombies. These were the ones, Isherwood thought, that hadn't been drawn northward by his gunfire.

He drove around a tall zombie wearing a tank top undershirt, denim shorts, and work boots. The zombie's reactions were slow, almost drunken. It didn't seem to notice the little green truck until they were almost right on him. It jerked suddenly, as the truck drew within fifteen feet or so. It almost hurled itself at the truck. Isherwood was surprised at its speed and ferocity. It seemed to erupt from a state of dormancy. It wasn't awake very long, however.

Micha didn't let the tank top zombie get anywhere close to his family or the truck. The thing's head exploded in mid-lunge, as Eli's shotgun exploded. Isherwood could just see, through the rear-view mirror and between Annie and Mary's heads, the satisfaction beaming across Eli's face. He must have watched helplessly through the camp's windows as the zombies staggered one by one to the camp, as they slowly surrounded it and trapped them. It had been almost an entire month now of helplessly watching and the slow agony of starvation. He could only imagine what Glenn must have felt watching his family slowly die from starvation and waiting for them to die, turn, and wake with vacant, hungry eyes.

Isherwood broke free from his musings at the sound of a second shotgun blast. It was Micah this time. He scolded himself for losing his focus. All this could be for nothing, including Marshall's horrific death, if he lost focus now. Not only that, there was the girl they had found in the Brooks Plantation . They had locked her in the troop transport truck with food and water. She could survive that way, but not forever. If she started pounding at the door in her madness, she could draw them in. They might return to find their getaway vehicles surrounded. He just hoped their captive wouldn't draw in a crowd from the interstate. This was unlikely, though, as the boat was still serving as a giant lure and diversion in the opposite direction.

Two more shotgun blasts erupted from the bed of the truck. The zombies were beginning to get thicker. Isherwood turned off the main north-south cut. The green truck turned into a gap in the trees and along a narrower trail that snaked in a southeasterly direction toward the Pilot Channel.

Dodging zombies on a trail this wide would be next to impossible. If they ran into a pack of any size, Isherwood would have to stop and clear the road, losing precious minutes. If there was a mob of any great size, they might need to reverse all the way out back to the cut. If the normal speed of the truck was any indication, the zombies might be able to outrun them driving in reverse. They had to take the chance, though.

Without a word from Isherwood, Eli and Micha seemed to understand the predicament. Isherwood caught a flash of a half-naked zombie through the trees on the far side of a curve in the trail. Before he was even conscious of its presence, Micha had picked it off. It must be easy for them, Isherwood thought. Their eyes are trained to see deer through the thick underbrush. With just a glimpse, they knew rack size, age, and distance to target. *And*, Isherwood thought, they could do all of this at an hundred yards or more. How much easier would it be for them to spot and shoot a brightly-dressed zombie at twenty yards or less? It couldn't be that difficult to overcome the muscle memory of aiming for the head instead of the lungs. *Right?*

*****

The woods suddenly fell away before the truck and a long tin-roofed shed appeared on their left. There were half a dozen ATVs stored there. "Those would've been nice to have a mile back." Isherwood grumbled to himself.

"Watch out," Missy said softly. Isherwood could see she was struggling to lift her right arm, as she pointed. He was relieved to see it, nonetheless. It was an improvement. She was pointing at a few zombies that lurched into the roadway from a stand of tall grass. Micah and Eli had dispatched both of them by the time she finished raising her hand.

Their blood chilled as a large, many-throated moan erupted ahead of them. The double shotgun blast seemed to have awakened a thickening crowd of zombies. They had finally arrived at the Pilot Channel. Clump by clump, the dark silhouettes of the zombies began standing out from the shadows under the trees and in the brambles. There must have been hundreds loosely scattered about. In just the few seconds since they had burst through the clearing beside the shed, the vice had already begun to tighten around them.

"Clear me a path!" Isherwood shouted through the back window. "I'm taking the road south along the Channel." Any vagaries he had had of stopping at the shed to trade out vehicles quickly vanished.

"Save your ammo," Isherwood shouted again. "Just clean up the road ahead." The thin metal roof of the cab groaned and buckled as Micah and Eli re-positioned to aim straight ahead. They were like two forward pointing horns on a charging bull. Isherwood just wished his bull had a little more horsepower.

The zombies began to fall away in sheets in front of the small truck, as it began its wide turn to the south. The road soon branched off and fell away into the Channel. This was the one and only, though somewhat crude, actual boat dock on the whole island.

After the dock, the road continued southward, Isherwood knew, for at least half a mile, maybe more. He hoped they would be able to find some sort of make-shift boat ramp, if they could only make it through the brambles and swamp between the road and the channel.

Though the boys were effectively laying down the zombies ahead of the vehicle, the dirt road was quickly filling with zombie speed bumps. The small truck lost a lit bit of speed each time it lurched over one of the piles of fetid flesh. They had to maintain some kind of momentum to pass through the swarm. They didn't have much speed to begin with and what they had was quickly wasting away. And Isherwood knew this crew wouldn't make it long at all on foot.

Isherwood caught a glimpse down the boat ramp as it passed along the left side of the truck. It was like a long pirate plank reaching down into the water. Dozens of zombies at a time were spilling into the Channel and lurching away into the swift current. Hundreds more were pushing at their backs eager to follow them into the water. The waves of zombies, he saw, were gradually slowing as a call to new prey was percolating down the ramp. They were, all of them, slowly stopping and turning. The desperate sound of the small truck's struggling motor was like a siren going off.

The back passenger tire suddenly caught on something – probably a rib cage or a femur jamming itself between the tire and the wheel housing – and the truck jerked backward. Isherwood gunned it, hoping to spin out of it. It did no good. The truck soon died. It lasted just long enough to drive them right into the thick of the swarm.

Isherwood took a second to cuss under his breath and grind his teeth together. He reached under where Annie was sitting for his swords. He had laid them along the floor boards. Before reaching for the door handle, he yelled some quick instructions into the radio. "Mayday! We're stuck at the boat dock! Mayday! Stuck at the dock. Come quick or not at all."

He swung the door open. He knocked over a pair of corpses as he did, giving him some space to get ready for the oncoming waves of zombies. He unsheathed the first sword and got to work. He left the other sword with the girls. He gave them quick instructions on how to push it through a small slit in the window, if any got close. Behind him, either Annie or Mary pulled the truck door closed again. They would be safe for now in the cab.

Micah and Eli had never stopped shooting. Their ammo was holding out for now. Though he had no time to turn and look, he was pretty sure Glenn was getting in on the action, too. His will was just too strong to be overcome by starvation.

There were fifteen or so zombies within ten feet of the truck. These needed to be cleared out first and hopefully before the first wave scrambled back up the somewhat steep and slippery dock.

Half a skull with the ear still attached flew down the ramp and skittered away as Isherwood brought the blade down through the first zombie. The katana blade sank deep into the zombie's shoulder, as well. The body slid off the blade on its own and the thing's arm fell as a separate, mouldering heap.

He shifted the angle of the blade slightly and drew it to his side before slicing it upward through the neck of the next customer. He let the force of the swing spin him into the neck zombie. A few seconds more had resulted in as many kills. Micah and Eli had cleared out the zombies that lay outside the swordsman's range. There were allowed just a moment to regroup and turn towards the oncoming wave of zombies from the ramp.

Isherwood sheathed his sword for the moment and switched to the 9mm pistols he had holstered at each hip. "Drop 'em in a line!" He called over his shoulder to his brothers-in-law. They might just be able to slow the advance of the zombies with a barricade, he thought. It might keep them alive long enough for the cavalry to arrive. Maybe.

Isherwood positioned himself a few feet before the center and top of the ramp. From here, he was basically shooting point blank at a seven or eight foot line of zombies. There were equal lengths of battle lines on either side of him, just enough for the brothers. Together, they dropped the first wave more or less neatly along the top of the ramp. The ground on either side of the ramp had eroded away enough to prevent the zombies from flanking their line. While waiting for the zombies to climb and stagger over their heaped-up comrades, Micha and Eli had time to knock off the zombies approaching them from all the other angles or to reload. Glenn, still laying prone in the bed of the truck, took care that nothing slipped through the cracks.

"Kinda like turkey huntin'" Eli said, as the stress of the moment began to slip away. "The heads just sorta evaporate in the shot."

Micha was focusing more on picking off the zombies at their flanks and back. The older of the two brothers, he had developed a bit of a perfectionist streak. He was distracted, waiting for a perfect shot on a zombie a hundred or so yards back up the road they'd come in on. In doing so, he was letting zombies breach the still-low barricade at the top of the ramp.

"Micha," Isherwood grunted as he swung through the cervical vertebrae of a black woman. She was wearing the muddy remnants of a long pink pajama shirt. "Pay attention! Your line is *breaking*." Isherwood had returned his pistols to their holsters after getting his line built up a little, trying to conserve ammo.

Suddenly, there was a hail of gunfire. Isherwood was about to turn and thank Micha for his renewed effort when he realized the fire wasn't coming from behind him. It was coming from the other side of the ramp. The channel side.

"Keep it up, guys. Just hold them for a little longer. The cavalry has arrived. Hopefully." Isherwood cheered down to his friends, raising his sword into the air. This was as much in celebration as practicality. He was covered in filth and didn't want to be mistaken for a zombie.

Justin and Patrick cheered back. Padre was driving the boat. He wasn't yet bringing the boat in too close. They couldn't tell how quickly the land dropped away past where the ramp disappeared into the water. Even if there was no land, the piling up off zombies could have formed the equivalent of an undead coral reef. If they weren't careful, the boat could be swarmed and brought down. Besides, they were diverting at least half and maybe more of the ramp zombies back into the water. This was making the situation atop the ramp much more manageable.

"Let's put these things down." Isherwood shouted over the roar of the gunfire to Eli and Micha. "Then, we'll start carrying your mom down to the boat."

He did not mention their dad, thinking that even now, he didn't want to offend the man's pride.

Isherwood began kicking against the sacks of rotting meat that formed his section of the barricade. He was trying to angle them outward to make a spot they could pass through. He sliced through the oncoming zombies so they would fall to either side of the gap. After another minute or so, the waves of zombies charging up the ramp had dwindled away. Isherwood finally turned away from his post to begin gathering up the women. He trotted to the far side of the truck, the passenger side where Missy sat huddled against the door. She had yet to recover any of her strength.

"Come on, guys. Help me carry her." Isherwood called to the boys.

"Okay, give me a second." Micha mumbled. He was still picking off stragglers on the ramp. Eli was beside Isherwood and then in front of him, as he tried to pull his mother from the truck. The strength in Isherwood's arms had mostly drained away after wielding the sword for so long.

"Micha, come help clear a path for Eli." Isherwood called again.

"A minute. Just another minute." The elder brother grumbled.

Eli was able to carry his mother with little difficulty. She had grown very frail and weighed very little. She wrapped her thin arms around her son's neck as best she could.

"Where are you going?" Glenn called out to Micha, as he lowered himself over the side of the truck bed. Glenn's voice was still very weak.

"Y'all go ahead." Micha called back. He, too, had left the relative height of the truck bed to wander off in search of more zombies. "I just can't leave this place a mess."

"We need your help over *here*." Isherwood insisted. "*Down* the ramp. Who cares about back that way? That'll take care of itself." But he was soon distracted by Annie and Mary climbing out of the truck. They were clinging to him very tightly. Mary had handed over Isherwood's second blade. Somehow, Isherwood noticed, Eli was carrying the bag of weapons in addition to his mother. Glenn, too, was carrying a load.

"All hands on deck, Micha – *come on!*"

Micha reeled around to face Isherwood and the others. His face was red with annoyance. Just as he was about to unleash a torrent of complaints at Isherwood and the others, a dark shape appeared beside the rusting hulk of a tractor behind him. He never saw it coming. His focus was on the zombies appearing at the edge of the clearing. That one could be so close never entered his mind until it was too late.

A second later, there was a terrible scream and Micha was standing speechless as the shotgun dropped clattered from his hands onto the wet ground. The creature never reached him.

Though she appeared only barely conscious, she must have watched the whole scene unfolding from just above Eli's shoulder. It had been Missy. She leaped from Eli's arms and threw herself the remaining twenty or so feet to the derelict tractor. She slammed her wrecked body against the zombie. It must have been every last ounce of her that she threw against that zombie. Because when the zombie started biting at her arm, she made no move to protect herself. She just stared helplessly up at her son. A small smile curled upward at the corner of her mouth.

Glenn, too, despite his weakened state, threw himself at the zombie now attacking his wife. He staked the butt of his pistol through the thing's skull. Next, brandishing a hatchet from seemingly nowhere, he hacked at his wife's arm above the shoulder. Within the merest moments, he had killed and removed the source of contagion. His wife just looked on without any pain.

In the blink of an eye, he had removed his belt and made a tourniquet around Missy's upper arm. He was on his feet and carrying her down the ramp before anybody had time to comprehend what was happening. "Come on!" He barked at the others. "Get on that boat."

The family galvanized into action. Eli grabbed his shotgun back out of the pack and began mowing down the zombies in his parents' path. Isherwood tossed the girls one by one over the barricade. Micha even gathered himself together, picking up his shotgun from the ground. There was simply no time to process what had just happened. That could all happen later, *if* they survived the next twenty or so feet.

CHAPTER NINE:

EVENTUALLY

The boat ramp consisted of a sheet of thick timber mats. The mats were the kind used to support cranes and were held in place by their own weight. They were slick with the gore of thousands of zombies that had passed this way before disappearing into the Pilot Channel. The place was littered with zombies whose bones had been crushed underfoot and pressed into the mud or the gaps between the mats. They would stay there until washed away by high water. For now, they would just be laying there helplessly groping and slowly rotting. Their mouths were snapping open and shut, like a bed of Venus fly-traps, as Isherwood and the LaGrange family came hurrying down the ramp.

Isherwood signaled to Micha and Eli to take point around Glenn, who was still carrying his wife, and the sisters. Isherwood went ahead of them down the ramp. He stood about ten feet from the water's edge. Many of the zeds were still trudging down into the Pilot Channel. Some were peeling away, however, and staggering back up the ramp towards the nearer prey. These were coming in a steady stream and Isherwood and his sword could keep pace.

The barricade they had made at the top of the ramp was now beginning to prove its worth a second time. Zombies, attracted by the sound of gunfire, were now filling up the clearing where they left the truck behind. If not for the barricade, dozens of zombies would now be sliding down the ramp. Even still, some were still coming over the small hill of bodies. On top of that, there was also the gap that Isherwood had made. In another minute, the ramp would again be full of zombies. Their small window of escape was rapidly closing.

"How you wanna do this, Isherwood?" Patrick called from the boat, which was only another ten or fifteen feet past the ramp. Isherwood took a quick look back up the ramp. His eyes met Glenn's and his huddled family and then darted away up the ramp to the oncoming hoard. He turned back to the boat, blinking as his eyes passed back over his wife's family.

"Throw me a rope," Isherwood shrugged. "You're gonna hafta cut the engines or they'll clog up with zombie meat." Patrick relayed the plan back to Padre. The priest cast a dark glance back at Isherwood and nodded.

Isherwood charged down the ramp as with raised bayonet. He did his best to clear off the last five or six zombies waiting there. Glenn had begun moving his family farther down the ramp by the time Isherwood caught the rope and began pulling.

The boat was no flat-bottomed pirogue. It was heavy and Isherwood had little to no traction on the gore-painted ramp. He slipped and fell hard on his backside. Luckily, he had already sheathed his sword or he might have bisected himself. He slide nearly right up to the water line. As he splashed into the water, dozens of fingertips began emerging from shallows. Just below the surface, his boots had found traction against a set of shin bones, the owner of which was stuck doing upside-down, underwater sit-ups. Isherwood regained his footing on the zombies' foot and ankle bones and began climbing back up the ramp with the rope over his shoulder.

"Watch out," Isherwood shouted between heavy gasps. He was now far past the point of exhaustion. "Watch out, they don't come up the sides," he panted. "We'll hafta push off with the rifles."

The sisters and Eli were already aboard by the time Isherwood turned back to the boat. Glenn and Micha were – as gently as they could manage – lowering Missy into Eli's arms. A hand reached out from the water and locked tight around Glenn's boot ankle as he was boarding. Mary and Annie responded quickly. They grabbed their father's shoulders and pulled. They both lost their balance and spilled into and against the swivel seat where Padre had been steering the boat. It had been enough, though. Glenn was all aboard except for one boot. Only Micha and Isherwood remained still on the ramp.

Micha, just as he had before, couldn't tear himself away from the oncoming zombies. He wanted to keep shooting. Luckily, his shotgun clicked empty just as Isherwood was trying to throw him backwards into the boat. Micha landed softly on the aft deck and sat there, trying to reload from his pockets, as Isherwood jumped over and aboard. Justin knocked Micha hard with the butt of one of his AR-15s, and the younger man gladly dumped his shotgun along the floor boards.

Hands were reaching out from the water along all sides of the boat. The water-logged flesh of the hands made terrible squeaking, sliding noises against the smooth sides of the boat. Glenn put up a hand as Padre moved to turn the engine key. The older man shook his head. "Wait." He said softly.

"Come on, help me." Isherwood grunted as he attempted pushing off from the ramp with the butt of a rifle. "Hurry, or one of us has gotta get out and *push*."

Soon, there were five men likewise pushing against the ramp, as zombies began spilling over the barricade and down the ramp. Annie and Mary had picked up spare weapons and were beating away the hands grabbing at either side of the boat.

The back of the boat suddenly lurched upward and rose almost a foot out of the water. A massive swell of zombie bodies suddenly lurched up from the submerged section of the ramp. The men pushing against the ramp from the back of the boat tumbled backward into the cabin. They were lucky it had not been the front section of the boat which had been lifted. All of them might have fallen overboard to be devoured by the thousand-mouth sea monster waiting below. As it was, the zombies helped dislodged the boat from the ramp better than the men could have done, even if they had all jumped out to push and perish. The boat was already drifting into the channel's current by the time everybody had disentangled themselves.

"What the hell was that? Zombie Jaws? Moby Dead?" Justin sputtered as he scrambled back to his feet.

"Our Lady of Prompt Succor." Padre prayed quietly. He had just called on her for help when the boat jumped out of the water and into the relative safety of the current.

"You stupid idiot!" Justin said, clapping Isherwood on the back. "You did it. The whole blessed lot of 'em. They're all here."

Isherwood gave a half-smile in response. "We're not out of Dodge just yet, buddy. But thanks."

"Yeah," Patrick sighed. "Let's see if we can start the engines."

Padre leaned over to face Glenn. "Any suggestions before I try cranking this thing up? It's been off and on, off and on a couple times already."

Glenn was helping his wife unwrap an energy bar he'd found somewhere in the boat. "Can't we just drift for a while? I haven't felt this safe in a long time." The man was smiling like an old fox.

"Eh – let's get going, okay?" Patrick muttered, suddenly nervous. "I don't want to get any farther from our convoy."

Isherwood waved his hand. "Don't worry, man. He's only joking. Have you ever seen a man more in need of a hot shower?"

Patrick laughed. "Uh-yeah. *You!*"

"He's right, dude." Justin said as he went to pat Isherwood's shoulder and then thought better of it. "You look like Carrie's prom date. Gross."

CHAPTER TEN:

MOBY DEAD

"Like a champ!" Isherwood shouted in triumph as the boat's engines roared back to life. Padre clapped his hands and slowly pulled back on the throttle. The sound of the water churning behind the boat was quickly growing louder and louder.

Mary sighed, "I'm just glad to hear something besides that constant moaning, moaning, *moaning*."

"Oh my God." Eli said, slack-jawed. He was staring up at the bridge beyond the pipeline. Zombies were still spilling over its sides. He raised a hand and pointed silently at the spectacle.

"I know." Patrick nodded. "It's crazy, right? We could sit here as bait for another week, and I don't think they'd slow down one bit."

"Get ready for when we drive under that." Isherwood cautioned. "It'll be raining men in no time."

Eli stared awhile longer. Still staring, he remarked, "They're ruining the whole island. Have y'all thought about blowing up the bridges on either side of the island? It *could* be, *would* be a good spot, if there wasn't this direct line to the cities."

The shadow of the pipeline crossed over Isherwood's face. "You're right," he said. He sat down in the back corner of the boat. "Eventually, I think we will. We'll need to start mapping out new territory to expand into. Places we could fortify or that have natural fortifications, like the island. The more survivors we find, the farther we can build out from St. Mary's. But always using the new location to help defend the center, St. Mary's. It will be a network of settlements expanding outward from St. Mary's. This way they'll be connected and mutually supported, and we can always fall back to the center." Everyone on the boat had gradually fallen silent as Isherwood spoke.

"Eventually, I think, the network of monasteries – that's our model, you see? The model will take us pretty far. We're bound to brush up against other groups trying to kick start society in their own ways, too. Good or bad. Our model will be tested against theirs. Eventually. But our model has been tested many times before."

Patrick laughed. "Did you ever think you'd end up a Founding Father?"

Isherwood shook his head in exhaustion. "Most Founding Fathers meet their *ends* at the end of a rope. Not exactly a good mortality rate."

"Heads-up!" Justin said, interrupting Isherwood as they neared the bridge. The falling zombies were now close enough that they could see their individual faces staring back at them. The men led the LaGrange family down into the boat's hold, packing them in except for Micha. Then, they all hurried backed under the protection of the fiberglass canopy of the cabin.

"Steer to starboard! To starboard – to the *right!*" Patrick began shouting. He saw what looked like a long white snake suddenly loom up from the depths of the Channel. "Did you see that? It was like an albino anaconda or something, but thick around – almost as wide as the boat."

"What?" Isherwood said. He hurried over to the side of the boat where Patrick had been standing as Padre steered them closer to the eastern bank.

"Not too far, Padre. If it gets too shallow, too quick that way, we're in just as much trouble."

"Ah, crap." Isherwood shouted, as something beat hard suddenly against the underside of the boat. Isherwood was nearly knocked overboard. "Ah, crap. I just saw it, too. Let's get out of here, okay? More speed, more speed."

"What the hell, man?" Justin said looking as Isherwood's face which looked very pale, despite all the layers of encrusted blood.

"It was, uh, they were all sorta bound together, you know?"

"What?" Justin repeated. "What were bound together?" He was feeling the panic rise in his chest, as he watched the fear grow in his friend's eyes – the same friend who had just walked a pipeline to hell and back.

"Zombies – what else? They must be holding onto each other as they're pulled downstream. It's like the limp neck of a dead Brontosaur – er, Brachiosaurus – drifting back and forth down there."

"Okay, I feel better." Justin said exhaling.

"Why?" Patrick said aghast.

"Because my boy, Isherwood, over here just took time to correct the dinosaur's name. Can't be that panicked, if he's thinking like that."

Their conversation abruptly ended as bodies began pounding against the boat.

"Faster!" Isherwood called out, as he pinned a zombie face down and plunged his sword into its skull. "Get over there before they start falling."

Padre mostly ignored Isherwood's instructions. He was having a hard enough time keeping the boat away from the bridge pilings in the choppier water under the bridge. Anything could be hiding in the shadows under the bridge. He didn't want to slam the boat into a hidden shoal of mounded up bodies.

"Don't!" Patrick called out, pushing the barrel of Micha's rifle aside. Micha had been aiming the rifle at a zombie he'd thrown down onto the deck. "Don't shoot that thing down through the boat. Are you crazy? Your family's down there!"

Micha shook his head as if he'd been caught in a trance. "Oh man, sorry. My bad." He stomped on the zombie's neck instead and quickly shoved his hunting knife into the creature's temple, instead.

This time, most of the zombies hadn't fallen in the boat and were deflected into the water. There were only four to contend with. Justin, Patrick, Isherwood, and Micha each picked a zombie, like it was a pickup game.

"Sweet," Justin was saying as he let the torso and then the legs of his zombie tumble over the side of the boat. "Mine was wearing a 'Feel the Bern' t-shirt. That was pretty satisfying. You got wonder, you know?"

"About what?" Patrick asked.

"How all those guys felt about gun control, you know, *in the end.*" Justin said, shaking his head. "Gun free zones must've been a feeding frenzy."

"Unless they were all zombies to start with." Patrick said with a wry grin.

"Heads up!" Padre interrupted them. They again took cover under the canopy and waited for the bodies to fall. There was a slap of meat against the canopy and then a splash.

Just before the meat started hitting the canopy, Isherwood thought he heard something. A voice. "Hey," he called, but no one noticed.

"That's it?" Justin interrupted. His loud voice easily overcame Isherwood's somewhat softer voice. "Just one? I don't like this. That was too easy. We're probably gonna have a Bingo Bikini Beach Blanket Party waiting for us back at the camps."

"Bingo what?" Patrick was saying.

"Easy?" Isherwood grunted. "Tell that to Missy and – man – poor Marshall." A wave of guilt rushed over him, and he completely forgot about what he had heard.

"Dude, you know –" Justin started.

"I know. I'm sorry. I'm just still cranked up. Like I've been living on caffeine for a few days. Look at my hands. This is just stupid."

Padre was nodding. "We need to get back and fast. This is a traumatized group and it's on the verge." As Padre was speaking, Isherwood glanced sideways at Micha. He knew something wasn't right with that kid. He had been pressed into some crazy situations, sure, but Micha's response was just off. He couldn't quite put his finger on it.

"Speaking of trauma," Patrick said. "We've still got that feral child locked up in the transport. God knows what we might be returning to."

"Yeah, let's just ditch the boat and get back on the land as fast as we can." Isherwood nodded.

Justin winced. "I hate to just beach this boat. It's a nice boat *and* it's an escape route if things go sideways on the land."

"If we see a good place to dock past where we parked, we'll take it. If not, we just go for it."

*****

About ten minutes later, everybody was back topside and preparing to make a run for the vehicles. "Just get the anchor line ready," Isherwood was calling out. "We can at least tether the boat to a tree or two, just in case."

"Whoa," Patrick said, as the boat pulled into view of the same beach they had only barely escaped earlier in the day. The sun was now dangerously low in the sky and threatening to disappear behind the trees. The backyards of the camps looked just as they had left them. The water was still unnaturally still, but the zombies that had dived in after them, they quietly hoped, must be long gone. One end of the little pirogue that they had ferried an unconscious Isherwood in was just peaking above the waterline. This gave them a reference point as to the depth of the water.

"Whoa," Justin echoed Patrick. They were amazed to see that the whole area was empty of zombies. The whole swarm must have migrated southward following the boat.

Isherwood was nodding approvingly, too. "Nothing on the land and I don't see any little fingertips reaching up out of the water."

"Yeah, let's just test that sentiment." Patrick said. He was reaching over the side of the boat with one of the rifles and tapping the surface of the water with the stock.

"Don't you think the boat's engines would've set them off if they were there?" Justin asked.

"Oh." Patrick nodded dejectedly. "Right." But even as he said it, the hands and heads started rising from the water.

Justin's eyes grew wide. "Weird. It *was* the paddle, not the engine."

The girls drew back in fear. They had been sitting along the side of the boat and now edged up closer to the captain's seat. Micha raised his rifle, as though preparing to fire.

"Whoa, dude. Hold up on that." Patrick said, gently lowering the barrel of the young man's rifle. "Don't want to draw in any more, right?" Micha nodded distractedly in response.

Isherwood was at the bow of the ship, holding what was left of the anchor line. He studied the submerged zombies for a moment. "Looks like it's only a few. Probably the ones too stuck in the mud for the current to pull away."

As he said it, Padre killed the engines and let the boat coast into the increasingly shallow waters at the back of the line of houses. They could now just make out the line of vehicles parked on the road beyond.

"Wow. This could've been *a lot* worse." Patrick said looking at the zombies that had gathered around their vehicles.

"There's only – I don't know – maybe twenty?" Justin agreed. "There's almost that many of *us*."

*****

Isherwood jumped off the front of the boat and charged up the bank, splashing through the shallows. He didn't seem too concerned about encountering zombies. His boots rose above the water level. He turned and began pulling on the anchor line as soon as he got a decent grip on the dry ground. His efforts turned out to be mostly futile. The boat was just too large from him to have much if any effect. He quickly realized this and began running the line to the closest, biggest tree. The trees weren't very thick this close to the shore, but there were three cypress trees growing not far apart. He ran around the copse of trees with the anchor line twice, ducking when he recrossed the line.

Padre and Justin began tossing the bags onto the shore, while Patrick helped Micha carry Missy to shore. The girls tried jumping over the last couple feet of water and nearly lost their balance, but Eli was there to steady them. He, too, was wearing high rubber boots.

By the time they were all ashore, Isherwood was beyond the houses and had capped the first zombie. The crowd behind him was beginning to draw the notice of the zombies surrounding their vehicles. They barely noticed Isherwood stalking up and into their midst. This may have been due, in part, to the layers of zombie filth that Isherwood was still covered in. He had neglected to wash himself off during the boat ride. After catching a glimpse of what was in the water, though, he wasn't about to dangle his arm into it.

A trickle of zombies was soon headed to the disembarking party. Isherwood was at the rear of it. He was soundlessly mowing down the zombies at the back of the line, like Gary Cooper in *Sergeant York*. There were only two zombies left, a lady in what was left of a pant suit and man with a mullet, by the time Isherwood had rejoined the group. Isherwood's blade relieved the dead man of his unfortunate hairstyle before putting his body to rest.

As Isherwood was sheathing his sword – both were now back in place across his back – he noticed the remains of the first zombie he had killed with the sword in this yard. He had sliced through its skull perfectly after Marshall's expression of fear had alerted Isherwood to its presence. Marshall had then found the keys to the boat in the man's pockets.

"Padre," Isherwood whispered. "You got the boat keys?"

"Yeah," he answered, nodding to a pocket on his cassock. "Why?"

"Let's put them back in here." Isherwood said pointing. "That's where Marshall first found them."

Isherwood looked back at Padre. Padre held his gaze and nodded.

"Come on, y'all." Justin grunted, holding a couple bags. "You expect me to do all this shepherding myself?"

They were all climbing the small hill leading up to the vehicles. Zombies were beginning to appear down the road. The sound of moans was growing louder from the direction of the bridge.

"Ah, come on! *Really?*" Patrick was calling out, neglecting to whisper.

A couple of the others shushed him. Isherwood and the rest of the original crew, though, quickly saw what Patrick was complaining about. Old Blue was *gone*. There was the troop transport still in the center of the formation with Isherwood's Jeep and Justin's Escalade parked on either side and the Humvee behind. But Old Blue, which always sat at the head of the line, was gone.

"Uncle Jerry is gonna be pissed." Isherwood was chuckling to himself. "But I'd much rather lose a truck than another person."

"Old Blue basically *was* a person, you jerk." Justin was struggling to deal with the moment. "Can't we have a moment to mourn him? For pity's sake!"

"We may yet see Old Blue again." Padre said as he opened the back doors to the troop transport. He held one hand poised over his sidearm. "He's probably just on a recruiting trip."

Padre looked inside the dark transport. The sun was now beneath the trees, and the light was quickly fading. The girl was still strapped onto the ironing board. As he climbed into the truck, he noticed that the food and water hadn't even been touched. The girl looked funny, though – not like she was sleeping. His eyes were slow to adjust as he stared at the girl's face. He shivered suddenly, as his eyes finished adjusting. She was staring at him.

Padre took the girl's arm. It was limp as though she was sleeping. He strapped the girl's arm back to her side. He reapplied the gag, as well as a cross of holy water on her forehead.

Moments later, the girls, Micha, Missy, and Glenn were all loaded into the back of the transport. Padre gave them all strict instructions not to unstrap the girl "no matter what happens." Isherwood decided to bring Eli, instead of Micha, along with him in his Jeep.

"But wait," Patrick said. "Who's gonna drive the transport now that Marshall's – uh, I mean –" He let his words trail off awkwardly. Between Padre, Justin, Patrick, and Isherwood, none of them really knew how to drive a truck that big.

"I'll do it." Glenn said. He suddenly seemed stronger. Maybe it was the food finally taking effect, or maybe it was again being needed. Before anybody could object, Glenn had climbed back out of the transport by himself. "Micha ride with me in the cab." He said, and that was the end of it. They quickly dispersed back to their vehicles as the next wave of zombies was suddenly upon them.

All the engines miraculously cranked back to life. Isherwood's jeep took the new lead spot in the convoy. All they could see now were clear roads ahead.

CHAPTER ELEVEN:

LIVONIA

"This is Isherwood. Anyone there? Over." *Click-shhh.*

After a long pause, the radio static chirped to life. "Ah, hey. Yeah. This is Le'Mark. I'll go get her." *Click-shhh.*

"Oh hey, buddy. Good to hear you up and about. No problem. Just tell 'em, we're on our way to deliver the package. Over." *Click-shhh.*

"The what? The package? Uh, over." *Click-shhh.*

"Sara's family. We're incoming and we've got the whole LaGrange family with us. Over." *Click-shhh.*

"Oh wow. Okay. I'll go tell them. They're all at the Rectory. Over." *Click-shhh.*

Isherwood led them north out of the Sherburne Wildlife Refuge and back east on Highway 190. He decided to avoid the side roads and drive as much on the highway as possible. He just wanted to get home. The strategic part of his mind was worn out. Besides, the sun had now completely gone down. Street lights no longer illuminated the roadway, though in Louisiana, there weren't many street lights to begin with. It was now very dark along the roadway.

They had avoided the highway on their way to Whiskey Bay, sticking to the side streets. They had spent so much of their time clearing roadways. The highway was actually much clearer than the side streets had been.

They were able to drive right in to Livonia. This is where Isherwood, even before the Apocalypse, would turn north to drive into St. Maryville. This is what he intended to do this time, as well. At least it was.

The headlights of Isherwood's Jeep suddenly illuminated a familiar sight. Even from a quarter mile or so away, he knew the vehicle's distinctive shape. He could almost still see the blue beneath all the black spray paint.

He continued another furlong or so, halving the distance to the truck, and stopped. The convoy formed up behind him. It wasn't just Old Blue in the roadway.

"Alright, now I understand why the roads are so clear." Justin said. He and Patrick had left the Escalade and were standing behind the Jeep with Isherwood and Eli. The rest were staying in their vehicles for now.

Just beyond the familiar shape of Old Blue, illuminated by the headlamps of all the vehicles was a wall of stacked cars. The vehicles were stacked like bricks in overlapping rows. The wheels and tires had been stripped off and most of the roofs had been collapsed for stacking. There was a gate of sorts blocking a hole in the wall. It was a reinforced eighteen-wheeler that seemed to serve as a portcullis.

"It looks like it's still unfinished." Patrick said pointing to a point on the wall just beyond where the headlights were shining. The wall there shifted from two cars high to three.

"Maybe the builders went the way of the zombie." Justin said.

"I don't know," Isherwood was shaking his head. "What about Old Blue? He didn't drive himself there."

"Weirder things have happened." Patrick joked.

"Probably what happened – whoever took Old Blue wanted to keep going and couldn't get past the barricade, so they climbed over or through and continued on foot. Or maybe found another vehicle on the far side."

"Hey," Padre said walking up to join the huddle. They looked to him as though expecting him to say something, but he just stood there silently.

"What'd'you think, Padre?" Isherwood asked. "What's the play?"

Padre looked to each of their faces which were sharply illuminated in the headlights of the troop transport. He seemed to be considered Isherwood's question. "We're all tired, right?" He finally answered. "What if we just call over to them? They might've just thought the truck was abandoned, like everything else in this world. They might even be potential allies. Heck, y'all might even be *related*."

Justin snorted. "The odds favor it 'round here."

"I think you're probably right." Isherwood nodded. "It's entirely possible the wall has been abandoned or, I should say, overrun. But cover me, alright?"

"Definitely," Justin said. He already had his AR at the ready.

Isherwood didn't walk too far. He kept behind the driver's side door of the Jeep. "Hello?" He said. His voice didn't come out clearly. He cleared his throat and tried again. "Anybody here?" He noticed out of the corner of his eye that a zombie or two were beginning to stagger out of the thick brambles beside the road. There was a railroad track that ran just south of and parallel to the highway. The headlights and the engine noise were bound to attract more. He sensed movement on the road behind him and guessed that either Patrick or Justin had gone to dispatch the zombies before their numbers began to grow overwhelming.

"That's close enough, buddy." A not-unfriendly voice called from the wall. "I'm guessin' you're sayin' we stole your truck."

"I'm not real upset about that, actually. I just figured you needed it more than we did – or thought it was abandoned." Isherwood answered. "I'm mostly hoping that you'll help us get past your wall. And –"

"You from around here?" The voice interrupted.

Isherwood paused before answering. He didn't want to give too much information away to a stranger. "Yeah, not far from here. I was actually just retrieving my in-laws from Whiskey Bay."

"Whiskey Bay?" The voice repeated. "You mean, uh – shoot. Hey, Phil. What's them folks' name down there?"

"You mean ol' Jimmy LaGrange?" A second voice answered.

"Yeah, yeah, that's him." The first voice responded. "They had a mess of 'em. The LaGranges. No, wait – *Jesse* LaGrange, not Jimmy. You know ol' Jesse, buddy?"

Isherwood nodded, wincing inside at how he'd had to kill what was left of the man earlier that day. "Of course. We've got his brother, Glenn, and his family with us right now. I married his daughter."

"Is that right?" The first voice laughed. "What's your name, son? I can't see your face with those headlights like that."

"Isherwood. Isherwood Smith."

"Shoot man. You know me, don't ya?" The first voice answered. "It's Tommy and Phil. We used to work for your daddy."

Isherwood laughed and clapped his hands. "Good Lord! Are you really? That was probably my Grandad, not my dad, but yeah. At the old Chevy place?"

"Yes, suh." The second voice – Phil – answered. "We knew yo' granddaddy real well. We was at the funeral. Back before all this, you know."

"Yes, suh. Mr. Charlie's son." The first voice – Tommy – echoed. "It's real good to see you."

"Look, man." Isherwood said. His thoughts were racing ahead of his mouth. "We're putting something together in St. Maryville. We're reinforcing downtown and St. Mary's is sort of our main base, you see? We've got sort of an outpost in Morganza, too. You see where I'm going with this? Is your site secure here? Where are we? Just west of Livonia? Penny's diner is just a few hundred yards down, right?"

"Yeah, uh." Tommy answered. "We're doing alright. Penny's is sort of our main place, too. We've got that and the hotel next door locked down pretty tight. There's about – what'd'ya say, Phil? People sorta come up on the highway, y'know? Fifteen of us now. We just lost one of the Davids."

"I'm sorry to hear that. I can't believe we didn't see any of this coming into Sherburne this morning – we took side streets and had to do a lot of clearing."

"See that!" Phil shouted. "I told you I was hearing something back over there. You said I was just crazy."

"Look, guys." Isherwood interrupted. "We can be pretty strong all together. If y'all get in a tight spot fall back to our location, okay? If we get in a tight spot, we'll fall back to here or Morganza – what do y'all think?"

"We'll see, I guess." Tommy said, changing his tone some. "It's been kinda rough for us, you see? That's why I came on your truck. We've been scrounging a lot. There's a lot of mouths to feed."

"Y'all doing any planting?" Isherwood asked.

"Hey, sorry to interrupt." Padre said walking up to stand at Isherwood's side. "But we need to either get going or get safe for the night."

"Hey, you that pastor from up in Morganza, ain't'ya?" Tommy asked.

Padre nodded without saying more.

"Right, like I was saying," Isherwood continued. "We've got that Morganza outpost. But Padre's right."

"Oh yeah, yeah." Phil and Tommy said in chorus. "We'll get that semi out of your way. You'll hole up here for the night, no problem."

A short while later, the convoy of vehicles had passed inside the wall. Penny's Diner was much closer than Isherwood had estimated. Tommy, Phil, and the others had obviously spent a great deal of time building a fortress along the roadway. The walls were at least two vehicles high all the way around. Unfortunately, Isherwood thought, it appeared that they had neglected their food supplies to accomplish the feat. Tommy and Phil showed the LaGrange family to a spare room in the hotel, but the others mostly fell asleep in their vehicles. They didn't meet the rest of the Livonia survivors until the next morning. Before falling asleep, Isherwood called over to St. Mary's on the radio, telling them to expect them in the morning, instead, as well that they'd run into a whole new group of survivors.

CHAPTER TWELVE:
THE RETURN

They arose with the sun the next morning. Isherwood had slept in the driver's seat of the Jeep. He was alone in the vehicle. Eli had joined his family in the hotel room. Through all the trauma of last couple weeks, he had grown used to sleeping in a single room huddled together with his family.

Isherwood pulled on the seat lever and lurched back upright. He saw now the full extent of the Livonia wall that Tommy and Phil had made. It was impressive. There were several acres within the wall and plenty of room to start planting. The wall was working, too. He caught signs of movement on the outer side of the wall where zombies had impaled themselves on rows of pongee sticks.

They met together with the rest of the Livonia survivors in Penny's Diner for breakfast. Penny's Diner was a stainless steel railcar-style building. It looked like a larger version of an Airstream motor home with its shining metal skin and rounded corners. A lunch counter stretched the entire length of the building and booths stood against the windows opposite the counter. Tommy explained that this was where he and Phil had originally taken shelter when the first swarm hit Livonia. Hands had beat against the glass and chrome for days, they said. They didn't know if it was the living or the dead hammering at their door. The swarm had just disappeared one night. Isherwood guessed that it had eventually joined up with the larger swarms wreaking havoc on the Interstate. They had peaked over the lunch counter the next morning to see the highway littered with the smoking wrecks of vehicles. They had been gradually expanding their footprint ever since.

"You mean you've done all this without any real guns?" Justin interrupted Tommy's story.

"People 'round here must've used up their ammo pretty fast. They is plenty of guns, but no bullets." Phil explained.

"They've basically survived on spears." Isherwood said to himself in disbelief. "That's just amazing."

There were a lot of familiar faces among the survivors. Several, they discovered, were survivors of the swarms flowing along I-10. These were not local.

Even in the midst of rapidly dwindling food supplies, Tommy and the rest insisted that the newcomers all join them for breakfast. They took the offered plates of grits and cups of water with gratitude.

Isherwood took particular notice of Missy as she was eating. She was obviously in a lot of pain and was holding what was left of her arm tight against her body, but she seemed to be growing in strength. Her skin was no longer looking as gray as when he'd first seen her. If she was infected, he thought, she would have started rapidly declining. It looked as if Glenn's quick thinking had saved his wife.

"Look," Isherwood said, taking his eyes off his mother-in-law. "We just can't leave y'all with nothing. We've had a pretty successful looting trip up to this point. I had hoped to bring the load back to St. Mary's along with all the entire LaGrange family, but maybe that was greedy of me. If we're all agreed, this is what I'd like to do." He explained that he would leave them with several of the buckets of dry food and seeds they had found at the Booker Plantation, as well as half of their supply of ammunition.

"But this is an investment, you understand?" Isherwood continued. "I'm investing in your as well as our own future." He turned around to a spot on the wall adorned with a large map of the area. It was yellowed and cracking at its edges. It had clearly been hanging there for some time. "I'm not gonna write on this because trouble may well come upon us one day soon. There will be other bands of survivors, and they may just want to take and burn, not rebuild – like *us*."

He pointed out St. Mary's, which was basically at the map's center, and traced a finger along the long, smiling crescent moon of False River and the sweep of the Mississippi River. False River had once been a part of the Mississippi River, he explained, but was now just a long lake. He showed them how the lake and the river almost made an island of the land around St. Mary's, except where the two no longer connected on the upstream and downstream sides. His group, Isherwood explained, had partially secured the land with their outpost at Morganza, which lay on the upstream gap between the lake and river, and by sealing off the Audubon Bridge.

"Y'all are here. Livonia. This isn't exactly the spot of the downstream gap between False River and the Mississippi, but it's pretty dang close. Do you see it? With this outpost, we can together seal up the space between the lake and the river. This is our most vulnerable side, though, because it faces Baton Rouge and the

Interstate. We have to take special care never to draw those swarms northward to our position, or we'll be overrun."

"Anyway," Isherwood said, noticing how fear and not hope was now spreading across the faces in the diner. "We're going to leave you with the means to protect yourselves, come what may. But promise be this – please, please promise me that you'll start planting the seeds we're leaving you with *right away*. Please start gathering whatever animals you can inside this enclosure. They are still cows you could gather up, I'm sure. If not, we'll start supplying you with what we can find, as well as chickens – though we may keep the roosters at St. Mary's. They get pretty noisy. Also, the bayou is just outside the walls, so it serves as sort of a moat – that's *really* good. Since the bayou is so close, though, it's another source of food. Tommy, you *love* fishing! Think of all the crappie and sac-au-lay you could be getting out of that thing."

By the time he had finished talking, the Livonia group of survivors had become believers. His dream had become their dream. They even signed a formal treaty with terms on the backs of two menus. The Kingdom of St. Mary's had formally annexed the Fort of Livonia by the terms of their mutual defense pact with "due and proper consideration given in the form of ten five-gallon bucks of seeds and rice, 1500 rounds of .22 caliber bullets, 1750 rounds of 9mm bullets, and one Chevrolet truck, formerly blue."

They also added a radio and batteries to the deal. The Livonia group promised to make contact daily at 10am and 6pm, weather conditions permitting.

"You're such a dork, Ish," Justin said shaking his head in admiration. "Yesterday, you were a ninja turtle and today you're Ben freakin' Franklin."

"Excuse me?" Isherwood said, clearly offended. "Of all the Founding Fathers, why that philandering, anti-Catholic, bald, scum—?" He said, trailing off into a series of indecipherable insults. The rest of the survivors started giggling amongst themselves. Their laughter soon grew in intensity as the weight and trauma of the last weeks seemed to, for the first time, melt away.

"Okay, now you're reminded me of Yosemite Sam. Is that better?" Justin said, adding fuel to giggle fit.

Isherwood nodded. "Much."

*****

As the top spires of St. Mary's church came into view, Isherwood squeezed the steering wheel of the Jeep until his knuckles turned white. He had led the convoy straight north from Livonia, up Highway 1. He knew he was slowly losing focus and putting everybody in danger, but he was just so excited to see his wife and children again, *especially* now that he had Sara's family with him.

"Did you ever think you'd see her again? St. Mary's, I mean?" He said, turning and asking Eli, who was still riding with him in the Jeep. Eli just shook his head a little. He seemed to be holding back quite a lot of emotion.

When the tall wrought-iron fences of the church came into view, he pounded his fist against the window with excitement. He had been dreading this. He just knew he would return to swarms surrounding the church yards on every side. Instead, there were only a few. The river must be going easy on us, he thought to himself. He knew that waves of zombies could appear suddenly as though belched up from the river, carried downstream from parts unknown. He planned to fix this just as soon as he could, somehow or another.

They had radioed ahead to let their families know they were almost home. As the convoy pulled into view, Isherwood and the others could see a small party had gathered together in the back parking lot of the church by the back gate. Uncle Jerry slid the gate open at their approach so they didn't have to stop out in the open.

The vehicles parked in a line along the back of the Parish Hall. Isherwood and Eli were the first out. Sara went first to her husband, as did the kids. Emma Claire and Charlie each grabbed one of his legs. Sara gave him a good, long kiss. "There's more where that came from," she said to him, grabbing his collar. Isherwood smiled dizzily, until his grandmother and aunt surrounded him.

"Gross," Eli said, as Sara turned to him and smothered him with a big sister-sized hug.

"Oh my God, Eli," she said, nearly suffocating the poor boy. "I thought I'd never see you – any of y'all – again." Tears were streaming down both of their faces now.

Sara and Eli met up with their father just as he was lowering himself down from the cab of the deuce and a half transport vehicle. Glenn hugged them both. Sara noticed immediately how weak her father had become. She thought she ought to go easy on him, but couldn't help herself. She hugged him so hard, she nearly knocked the wind out of him. Micha had snuck up behind her by this time to surprise her, which he did. Glenn and the boys then climbed into the back of the transport to help Missy out. Sara clapped her hand over her mouth when she saw her mother's missing hand and forearm.

Padre had also climbed into the vehicle to attend to the girl they had brought back from Brooks Plantation. Jerry and Tad helped him carry the girl into the church, and Monsignor followed slowly behind.

Gran ushered all the LaGranges as well as Patrick and Justin's families back to the rectory. She and Aunt Lizzy had been preparing a feast for them, Isherwood assumed, ever since they had first left.

"Breakfast was pretty meager at Penny's Diner," Isherwood explained to Gran. "I'm sure everybody is ready to eat."

"I'm just glad for the chance to return the favor to Glenn and Missy for a change. They've been keeping you and Sara supplied with all kinds of game and fresh vegetables for years."

"Thank you, Mrs. Lorio and Ms. Lorio. Truly." Missy said still cradling what remained of her arm.

Glenn was walking alongside Missy. "This will be the first real meal my family has had in probably an entire month. I'm sorry to say."

"My goodness," Gran said, shaking her head. "Isherwood should've left sooner. He always did leave things for the last minute."

At this, Isherwood and Sara exchanged smiles. "The Apocalypse might've changed the whole world forever," Isherwood whispered. "But it's gonna take a lot more than that to change Gran."

"What's that, Isherwood?" Gran said, cocking a sly look in his direction.

"It had been about a week without food when Isherwood found us. Longer for mom and dad, I'm sure, though they never let on," Micha explained. "I've never been so hungry in all my life. Those PowerBars you had for us, Ish. My God. They were probably the best thing I've ever tasted."

Gran led them in through the rectory's side door which led almost directly into the large dining room. Aunt Lizzy held the door open as they all trailed in. The LaGranges found that the table was already set for them. There was a place prepared for each of them. Gran had clearly had full confidence in Isherwood's ability to bring them all back. The LaGranges, however, had stopped in their tracks at the sight of the feast that was spread out before them.

"I never thought I'd see something like this again. Not in this world." Glenn said, as the food and candlelight reflected in his moistening eyes.

"We have quite the supply of food," Aunt Lizzy remarked from behind them. "Wait until you see the pantry. And the preserves – my God, the preserves! Wait until your morning biscuits."

"Is that Spinach Madeleine, Gran?" Isherwood asked. "Holy Mother of – "

"You just make sure our guests have served themselves before you set upon it, Isherwood." Gran scolded.

"This is like Thanksgiving dinner." Mary said. "Better even."

"We have quite a lot to be thankful for," Gran answered. "Maybe more than we've ever had."

The group spent the rest of the afternoon alternately eating and drinking coffee. And they never ran out of food.

CHAPTER THIRTEEN:
COFFEE AND CHICKENS

"So tell me more about this plan you have, Isherwood." Glenn said. His chair creaked in protest as he leaned back in it. Isherwood recognized that his father-in-law was now fully restored to former self. *It was probably Gran's coffee,* Isherwood thought to himself. Gran no longer used a coffee pot due to the limited supply of electricity, so all the coffee was made after the old style using a French drip.

The steam was still rising from their mugs and the earthy smell of coffee was thick in the air. Isherwood got up and placed his mug on the mantelpiece. As at the Diner, there just happened to be a large map of the parish at his back. An antique map hung above the fireplace of the rectory's dining room. An electric light hung above it which would've provided ideal illumination in days past, but now just hung there sprouting spider webs. Instead, Isherwood grabbed a candle from the table and set its brass base on the mantelpiece. The map depicted all the original land claims in the parish and pre-dated the Louisiana Purchase. The names of Isherwood's own ancestors – Gran's *great*-grandparents – were written in cursive along one of the narrow parcels of land depicted on the map.

As before, Isherwood showed the various approaches to their location. False River and the Mississippi formed sort of an island between them as they split apart and then come back together. "It's a lot like the island we just came from at Whiskey Bay," Isherwood explained. "Only the river and the lake are no longer connected." Glenn and the rest nodded in understanding and mild irritation. They felt like they had heard all this before.

He showed how the Morganza and Livonia outposts would protect the open lands north and south of St. Maryville. "Civilization can begin again right here, as it was cradled once before," Isherwood explained. "Right here in our own Mesopotamia – our own land between two rivers."

"But wouldn't an actual island be better?" Glenn asked. "Like the one at Whiskey Bay?"

Missy squeezed Glenn's hand with her one remaining hand. "I don't think I'll ever be able to go back there," she said. Glenn looked back to his wife. A sense of loss seemed to wash across his face, but it soon melted away as his gaze dropped to his wife's mutilated arm. He nodded and turned back to Isherwood.

"But," Isherwood said, not wanting to leave the topic so soon. "I have been thinking about the island. If it weren't overrun with zombies and if the I-10 weren't running across it, it could really be a good spot."

"No, it's fine, Isherwood. Really." Glenn said shaking his head.

"Sure, I get it." Isherwood said, looking to each of the faces at the table. "Returning to the island is the last thing that any of us want to do right now, but who knows what kind of situation we could be forced into at any second."

Seeing no protest, Isherwood continued. "The island could be made useful again *if* we did something about the interstate. If we blew up the bridge approaches on either side, we could seal off the island. It's like in that movie – you know, where they blew up the Brooklyn Bridge to seal off Manhattan island? Anybody see that one?"

"Oh yeah," Micha said. "Uh, that was – uh, Legend. *I Am Legend.*"

Aunt Lizzie frowned. "Sure it wasn't *Godzilla?*"

"No way," Justin was shaking his hands. "You're thinking *Dark Knight Rises*. They blew up like three New York City bridges in that one."

"Okay," Isherwood sighed. "So this apparently happens in *all* the movies."

"I think it was *World War Z*, actually." Patrick said suddenly.

"Whatever!" Isherwood blurted out. "You get the point. It could probably work for Whiskey Bay, too. But nevermind, we're getting *way* ahead of ourselves."

Justin tapped Patrick's shoulder and winked at him. "*No*, we're all thinking *28 Weeks Later!*"

Isherwood erupted. "That was freaking London! Okay? Obviously *not* Manhattan. And God help you if any of you say *Muppets Take Manhattan*. I'm gonna freakin' lose it."

When the red finally faded from his vision, Isherwood realized they were just joking with him. They were all still laughing, and Isherwood couldn't help but join in. "Jerks," he said, laughing.

"What the heck was I talking about, anyway?" He continued rubbing his head. "Gran, what'd'you put in this coffee?"

"I didn't put anything." A sweet voice came from the kitchen. "But your friends could've poisoned it, and I wouldn't have known, dear." Another round of laughter broke out.

Glenn finally put the group back on track, asking Isherwood what the plans were for tomorrow and the upcoming week. Isherwood thought for a moment as the laughter died down. "There is, actually, a project that I think you, Glenn, and maybe Justin, too, would be uniquely suited for."

"What's that?" Glenn asked. Both he and Justin leaned forward in interest.

"Bullets." Isherwood said matter-of-factly. "Ammunition. Padre's got about forty pounds of gunpowder stashed away in Morganza with all the other tools *and* a bicycle generator to boot. *And,* there's plenty more for us to scavenge from the Brooks Plantation. I think we should bring all of that here, where we're the safest — at least hypothetically. I wouldn't mind hiding caches of guns and ammo around the area, too. Justin, maybe you could be in charge of gathering up all these materials and getting them inside the St. Mary's fences?" Justin nodded in response. "Good, that'll be good. Once it's here, I'm sure that, between you, Glenn, and Padre, we can get the bullet factory up and running. In the meantime, Glenn, I'd like your help designing a way to make all the neighborhoods surrounding the church into pasture land — well, grazing areas. We could convert one of these actual houses into a chicken house. We have way more consumer goods and housing than we know what to do with. We need to find ways to make it all usable."

Glenn was looking at him with a note of suspicion. "Grazing cows in backyards sounds pretty radical, honestly. But, we'll see if this dog hunts or not."

"Great, that's all I can ask." Isherwood said excitedly. "Plus, we're gonna need all the domesticated animals we can find. Between the zed heads and being locked in their pens without food, I'm guessing we're already too late. But we've still got a shot at finding more cattle and chickens, as well as maybe some horses, pigs, ducks, etc. We could also try domesticating some of the wild stuff, like rabbits. We need it all, not to mention seeds. Or else, all of mankind's advances in agriculture could vanish within a season."

Isherwood watched as their eyes widened. Many of them had obviously not put Isherwood's drive to restore agriculture into the broader context. Glenn and Uncle Jerry were both nodding strongly. "This isn't just about eating, though that's obviously important. This is about every advance we've made since the plow. This is thousands of years of mankind's genius. We can't just let it all disappear."

"If you start bringing me more of those tractors from the John Deere store and even the Kubota dealership," Uncle Jerry said. "I'll make sure they're all maintained until we have use for them."

"The boys and I can start widening the walls to include more pasture land," Glenn added. "*And* start scouting out more livestock. But we'll need plenty of feed. We can bring in some loads of hay while we're at it."

"Just do your best to conserve the gas." Isherwood said. "We've got about seven gas stations in the area. We've been lucky so far. It was the cities that ran completely out of gas. Each of the stations is about half full, or so we've estimated. Actually, wait. No." Isherwood said, stopping himself. "Don't conserve the gas. The gasoline won't be good for anything in another month or so. Use it while we still can, let's have a burst of building, but conserve the diesel."

"About the feed, the chicken feed and the rest," Glenn began. "While it's still summer, we should hold off on using up whatever feed is available. Chickens can forage if they've got enough room, ducks, too, and the cattle can graze. We'll need to store up the feed come winter."

"Yes!" Isherwood said excitedly. "That's right on, Glenn. And what's more, I think this will be one of the harshest winters we've ever had."

"All the fires," Justin said nodding.   .

"Right. Exactly." Isherwood continued. "So much of the world we knew went up in smoke. Back when the plague was spreading like wildfire, it was utter chaos. People just straight up lost it. Whole cities burned down. All that ash in the sky – it'll be like when Krakatoa or whatever erupted back in the eighteen hundreds. World temperatures fell a couple degrees and weather was messed up for years. But this might be even worse. Remember the reports that were coming out of Afghanistan and Pakistan?"

"And China and Taiwan, too." Patrick added. "Nuclear bombs."

"Right," Isherwood said. "And the bombs we have nowadays – had – are exponentially more powerful than what they dropped on Hiroshima and Nagasaki. I wouldn't be surprised if we get *snowed in* this winter. Sara, *you'll* at least have cause to celebrate."

Her brow wrinkled first in confusion, but the wrinkles quickly melted away. "Snow scenes." Sara said, her eyes growing wide. Having grown up in Louisiana, Sara had come to think of snow as more of a legend than a reality. It was the stuff of elves and fairie folk, not real life. Glenn and Missy had taken the kids on annual summer trips to Colorado, when the snow had nearly completely receded except in the mountain passes.

"All I can say is, it may be a very long time until our species can live farther north than Louisiana." The thought hung heavy in the room. Isherwood was suddenly aware of the grandfather clock ticking away in the corner of the room.

Glenn pushed his ceramic dinner plate off his placemat, so that it rested at an odd angle. He leaned forward into the space he had created and crossed his arms in front of him. "Didn't you say something about zombies coming out of the river?" He asked.

"Oh, right." Isherwood sighed. He leaned back against the cypress wood mantelpiece, trying to get comfortable before he launched into the story. He wasn't able to find a perch fast enough, so Patrick launched into the story without him.

"The rags were waving like tattered flags along the barbed wire fences. That was the first sign that something was very, very wrong." Then, growing more excited, "It was just like a scene out of *MacBeth*. You know, 'Till Birnam forest come to Dunsinane' and all? Anybody? Nobody?"

After an extended pause where Patrick looked bug-eyed from person to person, Micha finally spoke up. "Oh, yeah, yeah. But you mean *Lord of the Rings*, right? With the ents or huorns or whatever at Helm's Deep?"

"Yes, *yes*. Thank you." Patrick said with relief. He had long been pained by classrooms of high school students who seemed practically illiterate. "Well, sort of. That's where that scene came from. Tolkein took that from Shakespeare, see?"

"Anyway," Justin interrupted. "Here's the important part. We figured out a strategy that day that saved all our butts and could turn everything around."

"Assuming we have enough ammo," Isherwood added.

"Right. Yeah, exactly." Justin said nodding to Isherwood. He then launched into a detailed description of their new strategy for mounding up the zombies.

"Oh yeah." Micah interrupted eventually. "Isherwood was doing that at the top of the boat ramp – using their numbers against them to make barricades of their bodies. It really works."

"Bet your butt it does." Justin nodded.

"So yeah," Isherwood jumped back in. "The river could just lay huge masses of zombies at our doorstep whenever. And that's pretty bad. This is a problem that we can solve with enough bullets and sturdy walls, but I'd rather find another way. I have something, which should at least help the situation, if not completely solve it. Maybe it can give us a little breathing room, anyway."

"Well?" Chelsea, Justin's wife, said. "What is it?"

"Don't you remember?" Sara smiled. "I was telling you about this."

Chelsea gulped. "Oh no. The chicken plan?"

"Oh, yeah!" Justin chortled. "The chicken plan. That's how we got the idea to dangle the boat *and ourselves* from the pipeline as bait. I remember now."

"You did what?" Gran and Sara interjected simultaneously.

"Nothing, nothing," Isherwood said, bowing his head.

Patrick rocked Isherwood back and forth by his shoulder. "Oh, I'm happy to tell this part of the story. Listen to this. Padre shot a grappling hook over the pipeline. Then, we let the boat drift downstream, see? Isherwood caught hold of the line. It was creeping upwards, pulled by the boat, right? He rode it up to the freakin' pipeline, like Barnum & Bailey or something. Then, he used that line to tie us *to the pipeline*. The zombies were just spilling into the Pilot Channel trying to get to us. It was the darnedest thing you've ever seen."

"Did you really?" Eli was staring up at Isherwood in awe.

Glenn was astonished. "*That's* how you got ashore. That's nuts."

"Mercy." Gran said, slumping down into a seat against the wall.

"So," Isherwood said, trying to move the conversation forward. His face had reddened in embarrassment and was now hot to the touch. He had never been very good with compliments or attention of this kind. "*So*, that's what I intend to do with the chickens in the river."

The heads of everybody in the room, even Sara who helped him think of the chicken plan in the first place, spun toward him, bewildered.

"Oh my," Gran said, sounding suddenly exhausted. "I think I'll just take my chances with the zombies."

CHAPTER FOURTEEN:

FENCE DUTY

P adre led morning prayer instead of Monsignor. Both were noticeably weary. Monsignor nodded off before the reading of the first Psalm. Isherwood scolded himself when he realized that he had forgotten all about the feral girl from the Brooks Plantation. Padre and Monsignor must have been up all night with her. He was slowly coming to realize that his own dreams had been disturbed throughout the night. There had been noises in the night that he had dismissed as dreaming. Animal noises.

The other side of the church, now mostly the LaGrange family, was seated together and reading from Psalm 91:

> "You will not fear the terror of the night,
> nor the arrow that flies by day,
> nor the pestilence that stalks in darkness,
> nor the destruction that wastes at noonday."

On his way to the main church building, Isherwood had noticed that a heavy concentration of zombies had accumulated at the church fences over the night. Now, he realized why. He was beginning to worry what they had brought back with them. *She might be sort of a beacon for the dead*, he thought grimly. *God knows how far those noises traveled. Or even* how *they traveled.*

Isherwood's side of the church took up the next round of verses, reading together:

> "A thousand may fall at your side,
> ten thousand at your right hand;
> but it will not come near you."

They must have finished the job, Isherwood thought. *At least for now.* He wouldn't notice until breakfast that Gran was absent from prayer. Monsignor had asked her and Aunt Lizzie to attend to the feral girl. They had been waking her up every few hours to feed her broth.

About this point, Isherwood began to notice the words of the Psalm being read. Padre, he figured must have picked the Psalm based on his night's work. Isherwood's side of the church was again reading together:

> "Because you have made the Lord your refuge,
> the Most High your habitation,
> no evil shall befall you,
> no scourge come near your tent."

The LaGrange family took up the response. They were on the right side of the church, as one faced the altar. The family typically sat on the left side of the church, but had shifted for some reason. This side of the church was lined with stained glass windows depicting the Joyful Mysteries, while the left side, the side with the tabernacle, had windows depicting the Sorrowful Mysteries. The Glorious Mysteries stood tall above and behind the altar before the roof sloped into a dome. The Resurrection window had been donated in honor of Gran's aunt, an Ursuline nun named Sister Saint Vincent de Paul who had died nursing to the infected during the influenza epidemic of 1918.

> "For he will give his angels charge of you
> to guard you in all your ways.
> On their hands they will bear you up,
> lest you dash your foot against a stone.
> You will tread on the lion and the adder,
> the young lion and the serpent you will trample under foot."

Isherwood suddenly realized then that this was no ordinary Psalm. It was an *exorcism* Psalm. This was likely not the first time it had been read in the church this morning, either. He took heart at the words and repeated them in his mind, *trample the serpent under foot.*

Good God, Isherwood thought to himself. *What is about to happen?*

*****

Gran and Aunt Lizzie were absent from breakfast, and the breakfast menu was noticeably altered. Aunt Tad had taken over kitchen duties. She had made a traditional LaGrange breakfast in honor of her brother, Glenn's, homecoming.

Isherwood was poking around at his breakfast, as were many of the others. "Egg gravy," he whispered to Justin, Patrick, and Padre. They were all staring at him in expectation of an explanation. Their grits had been served topped with brown gravy. Raw eggs had been dropped into the brown gravy to cook. Justin kept lifting up bits of egg in his fork and letting them slop back onto the pile of grits in his plate. He did this while staring at Isherwood in silent scorn. Glenn and half or more of the LaGranges were oblivious to all this as they devoured their breakfast. After Gran's feast from the day before, Isherwood just wasn't desperate enough to eat the egg gravy. He scraped the gravy and egg fragments to the side of his plate and ate the grits. He knew that today was going to be a busy one. Lunch would be a ways off and probably consist of only a Power Bar and water.

They had decided that Glenn and Uncle Jerry would work on the livestock and wall-building projects. Jerry would show his brother-in-law the progress of their farming operation, as well. Justin and Padre would start work on machining ammunition. Padre felt the need to check on his post at St. Anne's, as well, and needed to bring word of Marshall's death to those that remained. Micha and Eli would be loaned to Isherwood and Patrick, who were to start searching for barges or other watercraft that could support coops for poultry. Isherwood's chicken plan was about to be tested.

But first, the walls needed to be cleared.

*****

By this time, they all had assigned wall sections. It was best that they were evenly distributed along the walls when they came out from cover. Most of them were assigned to short wall sections near the church, where most of the zombies tended to congregate. Those that were better runners were assigned longer sections of fence behind the Church Office and the Adoration Chapel and around the back lot. They mostly used hunting knifes to stab the zombies through the iron bars of the fences. Some of the shorter people used machetes or homemade spears that they plunged upward into the skull through the neck and behind the jaw.

Scattering everybody around the fence prevented too much weight from being pushed against any single section of fence. It also kept the zombies from shifting around the fence too much and getting overly agitated. The ladies had developed this process while the men had been away. They found that a quick wall-clearing resulted in less moaning and less moaning meant less zombies to clear the next day.

95

Isherwood, Sara, Aunt Lizzie, and Gran were all assigned to the same section of fence. This usually meant Sara cleared the fence herself, as Gran and Aunt Lizzie were usually busy taking care of the little ones. Gran and Aunt Lizzie were gone again today, too, tending to the feral child that Padre and Monsignor had spent all night exorcising.

"The zombies really do most of the work for us," Sara was explaining the modifications they had made to Fence Duty to Isherwood. "They press their ugly little faces so hard against the fences. We've even found a couple that have actually squeezed their heads through the bars."

"That'll probably start happening more and more as their skulls soften with rot." Isherwood added.

Sara winced at the thought. "Gross."

"Yeah, we'll need to reinforce the fences for sure. If they get soft enough or if rain or body juices start acting like a lubricant, they'll start squeezing through the fences like those old Play-Doh toys. They're strong. They could even rip their torsos from their—"

"Okay, stop." Sara said, laughing despite obvious discomfort. "That's just – it's grotesque."

"Yeah, well. The memory will stick that way. You can never have too big or too many fences these days." He stopped to watch his wife for a second. He admired how proficient she was with the long hunting knife. Despite being shorter than many of the zombies, she stabbed downward and overhanded. He watched as she squared up in front of an especially hairy zombie. The zombie was bald on top, but more than made up for this in facial and chest hair. The zombie was shirtless with a prodigious belly. The rigor mortis had apparently further softened the man's belly fat. The zombie was pushing so hard against the bars that it was squeezing its belly into three sections. The skin had torn and fat was dripping down the wrought iron bars as a thick black ooze.

Sara brought her arm back and slammed it down through the temple of the thing's bald head.

"Nice," Isherwood said. "But you see what I mean about the Play-Doh spaghetti machine? The belly, huh?"

"Just – don't." She responded as she averted her gaze from the zombie's belly as it slid down against the bars.

He laughed and grabbed her from behind. "I sure am glad to be back home." He said nuzzling the space between her neck and shoulder.

"Don't," she said, trying to wriggle out from his grasp. "I'm sweaty and it stinks of zombie."

"I really missed you, even though it was just a couple days." He said and kissed her before letting her go.

"That's sweet," she said and batted her eyes at him.

After slamming her knife down into another zombie, a teenager wearing a high school sweatshirt and gym shorts, she turned back to Isherwood. "You have to leave again, don't you?"

"Me?" He asked, somewhat dismayed. "No – I – well, just for the afternoon. Why?"

She shook her head, looking down and putting her hand subconsciously to her belly. "Just a feeling."

"Oh no, those feelings of yours."

"Don't just dismiss it like that." She said, turning back to the fence.

"I wasn't!" He said as though hurt by the presumption. "I was trusting it and dreading what you might be ... what's coming."

She smiled at that, though Isherwood couldn't see because her back was turned. She grunted as she rammed her knife blade into another skull.

"Wait a sec." Isherwood blurted out. "Did you just see that?"

"See what?" Sara said as began moving down the line. There was a large gap before the next zombie. It was a twenty, maybe thirty-foot section of fence that was tight against one of the buildings behind the neighboring Poydras building. Their section of the fence was basically the entire western side. It rarely had many visitors since it was the side farthest from the church building. Even Jerry's tractor barely came out this far.

"That zombie you just skull-tapped ... did you see him?"

"I saw that one of his eyes was gone, but that was about it."

"Not just gone. It was an empty socket. Like it had a glass eye, right?"

"Yeah, but ..."

"I think I ... *yeah*." Isherwood said, peering at the crumpled mound of corpse at foot of the fence. "You see that shirt?" He said, pointing. He knelt down and pulled at the thing's shirt. It was a work shirt, white with blue lines. There was a nametag sewn onto the left breast pocket.

"Roger Workman?" Sara asked with a grunt of irony.

"'Monty', but nice."

"Well? I see your mind spinning about something. What is it?"

"This guy. I recognized him, sorta. He had a glass eye when I saw him last, but that probably went by the wayside pretty quick." Isherwood was shifting the corpse around from inside the fence. He pulled up on its shoe. The other one shoe was missing and not much remained of that foot. "Look at this shoe or the other foot. Actually, no – don't look at the other foot. See the tread? Almost completely worn through. Even parts of the sock have worn through."

"Okay, so? I get it. He's done a lot of walking."

"Yeah, but not walking around here. He didn't work *here*. He worked in Baton Rouge ... at the mechanic's shop *downtown*."

"So what? He made it back home and was still in his work shirt when he got bit. Or, he was driving home and never made it."

As she said it, Isherwood was pulling at the man's belt. He rotated the corpse a bit, so he could reach into the man's back pocket. He fished around for a second and eventually retrieved the man's wallet.

"Where did he live?" Sara asked with dread.

"Gonzales. Pretty much the opposite direction from St. Maryville."

"You're saying he walked all the way here from downtown Baton Rouge? Why?"

"Pretty much. The attacks came hard and fast downtown. Pretty much ground zero. If you're wearing a downtown work shirt, you probably died downtown. But a mechanic would have had a better chance of getting out, maybe hotwiring a vehicle, and then coming this way. It's nothing definitive, but still weird that I'd recognize him. I don't take coincidences like that lightly. It could explain why the waves of dead just keep coming."

"The River Dead explain *that*, don't they?"

"Only partly. The River Dead are always water-logged – flesh about to slough off – but not this guy. His flesh is even a little desiccated. It's not a good sign. BR is pretty much – I mean, it must be – a boiling cauldron of dead. Hundreds of thousands. The Mississippi is a great barrier, but the bridges are intact. Must be. Probably, hopefully clogged up by now, but even a trickle could be bad."

"We actually don't see a lot of those soggy ones, come to think of it."

"Their range is more limited than the dry ones, but that's not a rule to live by." He said, standing back up and exhaling heavily.

"Now what?"

"What?" Isherwood asked innocently.

"That sigh. I know that sigh. What're you thinking *now*?"

He smirked and shook his head. "You know all my tells."

"Yeah, so?"

"It's just that … that we'll probably need to seal off those bridges eventually."

She tried not to, but couldn't stop herself from crying. It was just a soft sob. Before he could move over to her and try to comfort her, she shook it off and wiped her eyes. "Yeah, okay. But not *tonight*."

CHAPTER FIFTEEN:

TRANSMISSIONS

Le'Marcus, Vanessa's boy, was running up to them as they rounded the corner of the church office, heading back from fence duty. "What is it?" Isherwood asked.

Le'Marcus was spitting out words as fast as he could. He was out of breath and had apparently forgotten in his rush which section of the fence Isherwood had been assigned to. "Radio – message – two different 'uns—"

"Whoa, slow down, man. Catch your breath. We can wait." Isherwood and Sara fell into step behind the boy as he motioned for them to follow. They didn't have far to go. They had already been rounding the corner of the church office. There had been a flower bed of mums and several stands of ferns and ornamental grasses between the sidewalk and the brick walls of the church office. The mums were looking pretty crispy, Sara had been thinking to herself before Le'Marcus surprised them. They crossed the patio between the Adoration Chapel and the front doors of the office. They were made of thick plexi-glass, Isherwood observed as he passed through them. They might have served the survivors well, he thought, if not for all the building's windows. He doubted they would last too long in a siege.

They turned into the long, horseshoe-shaped hallway which passed through the center of the entire length of the building. There were still plenty of spare rooms in the building. Vanessa and Le'Marcus' room was one of the few occupied, or even being used. The radio room had been set up in the room next to Vanessa and Le'Marcus' room. It had once served as Ms. Sandra's office, Isherwood remembered. She had been the church secretary for longer than he had been alive. He hadn't yet seen her wandering the streets of St. Maryville with the other "cut men," as Lucy called them. He was glad for that. It was still so odd for him. *Who would have thought*, he would sometimes wonder, *that I'd one day be stabbing screwdrivers and swords into the heads of so many people in this town*. It made him question who the real monster was.

"Two messages, sir. Two of them!" Le'Marcus was still saying as he pushed Isherwood into the radio room.

"Vanessa?" He asked. "What's going on?"

Le'Marcus' mother turned to him from her equipment. The expression on her face was a relief to Isherwood. It was somewhat relaxed, but still lined with concentration. She watched the anxiety melt from Isherwood and Sara's faces, and she smiled. "Oh, we had you worried? Nah, no. No emergencies. Well, first, Livonia has checked in a couple times. They wanted me to tell you, especially Mr. Tommy, how thankful they were for the food and ammo. They didn't want to worry you but they have noticed an increase in zombies coming from the south since you all passed through."

Isherwood winced. "I was afraid of that. Tell them to conserve their ammo and to clear out the zombies at their walls with their spears and knives. The gunfire will only draw more."

"Sure, sure," Vanessa was nodding. "They know to do that."

"Thank God," Sara said. She had noticeably tightened her grip on Isherwood's arm, as they stood side by side in the doorway of the radio room. "I thought you were gonna say they were or were about to be in a bad way, and that would mean ol' Ish would be off again."

Vanessa was nodding with a look of compassion on her face. She pulled Le'Marcus to her unconsciously, despite his resistance to the gesture.

"You – I mean, Le'Marcus – said there were *two* messages, right?" Isherwood asked, growing impatient.

"Oh, right." Vanessa was nodding. "There was. It was cutting in and out, you know.

"Right. Well, what'd'you make out?"

"Something – someone – out of Baton Rouge, some sort of group that just escaped the city. They just made it over the bridge."

"The new bridge?" Isherwood asked. Locals called the two main bridges in Baton Rouge the 'old' and the 'new' bridges, meaning the Highway 190 and I-10 bridges, respectively.

"Nah, no. The old bridge. They're coming this way!"

"*Our* way? Or Livonia way?" Sara asked. "Livonia seems like a straight shot for 'em. They'd have to take Bueche Road to come our way. How would they know the side roads so well?"

"I know, but no – they're coming *our* way." Vanessa insisted.

Isherwood eyed her suspiciously. "You talked to 'em?"

She looked down, suddenly distracted by the headset she was holding in her hands. "No, the reception was – nuh-uh. I think they probably heard, you know, our daily broadcasts, is all."

"That's fine, Vanessa. That's fine. You did what we agreed on. That's fine."

"Well, how'd they sound?" Sara burst out. She was wrapping her arms around herself tightly. Isherwood could see her chin beginning to quiver. He rubbed her back in comfort.

"This is it, honey. *The risk of civilization.* We have to take it, but that doesn't mean we have to trust it." He paused, thinking. "We'll send a small crew to Livonia, for now. But I'll go out and intercept the newcomers. If they pass the sniff test, we'll ask them to continue with us on to Livonia. If not, well. We'll do what we've got to do. What we've *got* to do."

EPILOGUE: WILSON

To any *alive* person that might be watching, the man's little ruse was obvious. He was bedecked in a yellow, thick rubber pancho. His weapon protruded from his right sleeve, but otherwise his whole body was covered in bite resistant material. Even so, he wouldn't have lasted any time on the interstate if he hadn't been covered in zombie entrails and smears of rot.

He looked every bit the bad-ass, but underneath the pancho's hood, his nostrils were quivering in agony. He was humming to himself to try and distract from the constant waves of heat and putrescence rising up from the concrete.

"Ahh! Seriously?" He complained to the interior of the pancho as gore exploded from a patch of entrails he had stumbled into. He was wearing tall white shrimping boots, so the splash of black ooze didn't affect him much. Nevertheless, a folded square of a moist towelette emerged from inside the pancho and began dabbing away.

A couple zombies nudged him as they passed him by. A green algae-covered one hovered for a second, sniffing. The zombie had likely been buried in the swamp for a time before changing. If it weren't for the layers of fetid scum covering what remained of its chewed-up body, it might have noticed the lemon-fresh scent of the towelette, but Wilson was lucky. As it was, the hoard of zombies kept moving around and past him, eastward long the interstate. Usually, the zombies just shambled about the interstate without a common purpose or direction, but just now,

Wilson had noticed, something had them moving. He had first noticed the strange behavior several miles back.

He had been in Grand Coteau, a small hamlet north of Lafayette, when everything fell apart. He was pretty well accommodated back in Grand Coteau. He had fortified a wing of St. Charles College there, where, until very recently, he had been a seminarian. The college had been surrounded by a sturdy fence, which also enclosed nut and fruit orchards. It was even the spot of an old dairy. In times past, the Jesuits had risen early in the morning to milk the cows. It was how the college had supported itself. The dairy barn still stood and a herd of cattle was still leased to graze across the grounds. They were still grazing for all Wilson knew. The summer grass would be plentiful for a long time yet.

Nevertheless, he had left it all. He told himself that he preferred to live along the open road, but he knew that was a lie. He had become lonely very quickly, after burying the last of his friends. As much as they repulsed him with their runny noses and endless germs, he needed people. He needed them and so was in search of them.

He had been walking for days. Driving just wasn't an option on the interstates north and east of Lafayette. Even if wrecks and abandoned vehicles hadn't blocked most of the road, there were just too many zombies. The hardest part of walking alone had been cutting open the zombie that had loaned him the intestines. He had actually vomited into the corpse's opened body cavity.

When he reached Interstate 10 north of Lafayette, he had looked west to Houston and East to Baton Rouge and New Orleans. In the end, he had chosen New Orleans. He was a Jesuit novice after all, and his province's headquarters were just outside the French Quarter. He might as well head that way, though God only knew what sort of nightmare might be waiting for him in a city the size of New Orleans.

It had been easy enough going. There were plenty of gas stations along the way, where he could fill up on sealed packages and jars of food. There were also plenty of moist towelettes in these places to refill the little supply bag that he had slung under one arm. Nearly every other car he passed had at least one twenty-four pack of bottled water stacked inside. He often had a choice between Poland Springs or Ozarka or Kenwood Springs.

As he pushed farther east, the gas stations began to fall away before the vast Atchafalaya swamps and forests. He at least was aware of this, having past this way before, though he had never paid much attention to the swamps before. They had been merely the green section of roadway between him and where he was going. Now, he was beginning to wonder if he hadn't been short-sighted in his packing. He had snatched a roadmap at the last Exxon, but he had kept his pack light. He was banking on a neverending stream of gas stations to follow the roadway, but he was finding that the few exits off of I-10 in the Atchafalaya basin were undeveloped and sometimes led to asphalt roads that turned quickly to gravel roads.

He was passing alongside a Volvo station wagon. He let his fingers rub along the side of it as he passed, as he always did. It was one of the man's many compulsive habits. He noticed, as he had a hundred times before in other cars forever parked on the interstate, that the driver of the Volvo was still banging around inside. It was a man – a father, by the look of it. Wilson turned away quickly when he saw the child seats in the back seat. He focused instead on the driver. He was still clutching a can of Campbell's Chunky soup. Wilson could see that the can had been gnawed at. It looked like the man had been able to open the other scattered Campbell's Chunky soup cans with his teeth, but not the last. As he passed, he saw that the man was missing most of his teeth and that the soup can was covered in dried blood as well as gnaw marks. The man was banging the soup can against the window as Wilson passed by. Wilson pitied the man, or what had once been a man. He thought the father, for all he had tried to do to save his family, deserved better than a purgatory of can banging.

But Wilson knew he had to keep moving. If he stopped, he knew, entrails or not, he would be swarmed. Even if he did dispatch the father soundlessly, he knew he would feel compelled to put the children out of their misery, as well. He knew this for certain, because he had been unable to stop himself from doing just that at the first dozen or so station wagons and minivans he had passed before even reaching Lafayette. He had even tried burying the first couple of families.

Despite all the wasted mental energy spent deliberating, his OCD took over in the end. It was always so. A line of cars stretching endlessly behind him bore the mark of the former seminarian.

His weapon was a steel-tipped pole that a crucifix had once screwed onto, the same one the altar servers had processed into and out of Mass holding. He had modified it slightly to fit its current use.

There were really only three motions required when he went about his business: stabbing a zombie at eye level, waist level, or on the ground. He had done each of these three motions now thousands of times, so his movements had grown very efficient. There was no wasted movement. Everything was streamlined for power and quickness. If it weren't for the momentary sound of glass breaking, there would have been no sign at all that he had made what he called "the sign of peace." Even the nearest zombies barely twitched in the direction of the car. Remarkably, the tempered glass of the window didn't break into a million little pieces, but bore only the single hole. This was how Wilson preferred it. He hated leaving a mess.

*****

Wilson had been noticing the increasingly odd behavior of the increasingly dense groupings of zombies, the farther east he traveled on I-10. They were growing less and less aware of him. They barely noticed him at all since he was covered in zombie gore, but he could tell their collective attention was focusing elsewhere.

Fine, he thought, *let's get a little extra exercise.* He flipped a switch in his mind, releasing his OCD from confinement. It felt like the long petals of a flower unfolding from the tiny calyx. He began methodically administering the "sign of peace." He approached the zombies soundlessly from behind, and they were never the wiser. After a couple more miles, the zombie traffic became bumper to bumper. The highway was clogged with zombies. Wilson was mowing them down like lines of kernels on a cob of corn.

He guessed that he had "peaced" about a solid interstate mile of zombies before his arms stopped working. He fell back from the crowd of zombies and unslung a small package from within his pancho. It was a nylon parachute hammock. He looped the ropes through the openings of the interstate's concrete side walls. He barely looked over the side before tossing his hammock over. The interstate stood about thirty feet above the water-level of the swamp. He had tied the ropes so that, once inside the body of the hammock, he could lower himself to a few feet below the bridge deck, completely invisible to any passing zombies.

When he had started his road trip, he tried sleeping in vehicles and then under them. He had lasted less than a minute trying to sleep under a vehicle. He had laid down first on his back staring up at the engine. He had tried turning over onto his belly and had nearly wedged himself permanently underneath a Toyota Camry. When his face was finally nose down on the asphalt, he became aware of the twin trickling rivulets of gore, meandering past either side of his face. He had left that place thirty minutes later, leaving behind a medium-sized pile of empty foil-lined moist towelette packages.

He acquired a hammock shortly thereafter. Slinging the hammock high up in trees was perilous, and not just because of the height. He had awakened many times in the early morning to find a crowd of frenzied zombies reaching up to his hammock, as if worshipping Wilson as some pagan idol. The first time this had happened, he was hammocked in a tree which stood alone in an open field. Luckily, it had been a live oak. He was able to climb down along one of its long branches before diving into the edge of the crowd of zombies. He had tucked and rolled like a champ, surprising himself that he didn't break an ankle or femur.

Wilson settled down into his hammock for the night. He had removed his intestine-covered pancho before nestling into the hammock. He hung the pancho from a hook at the foot of the hammock and laid back holding his spear across his chest. Despite his exhaustion, he ate only a small dinner. His supplies were running dangerously low.

Mowing down all those zombies had been more exhausting than he realized. He slept late into the following morning. The shade underneath the interstate and the overhanging canopy of trees kept Wilson in the dark long after the dawn. He might have kept on sleeping, but for a sudden eruption of sound.

His eyes snapped open at the sound. He had almost forgotten what man-made noises sounded like. He sat bolt upright and was lucky he didn't jump right out of his hammock. "What the —?" He shouted out loud, forgetting himself. It didn't matter, though, because the sound began repeating. Neither the living nor the dead would notice him so long as that sound kept ringing out.

After a moment of panic, Wilson recognized the sound of the fog horn. He also noticed that it was blaring at irregular intervals. It was likely not some sort of automatic alarm, preset to go off on a, now outmoded, schedule, or even the death rattle of chemical plant about to explode.

The idea was slow to dawn on him. The sound, if not mechanical, must be *man*made. *Finally,* he thought. *Survivors!*

He had heard other noises that he thought might've been survivors. It might have just been the phantom sounds of a lifetime spent among people. He had caught glimpses of other survivors, but they had all run from him. Some, he thought, had been children that had become feral, probably the result of extensive trauma. Wilson had studied psychology before entering the Jesuits, not that it was all that useful anymore. *If it ever was,* he thought.

Wilson scrambled out of the hammock and back over the side wall of the bridge. He leaned his spear against the concrete wall, as he gathered the nylon parachute material and the pancho still hanging at one end. The zombies at his back barely noticed him in their frenzied rush towards the fog horn. This was fortunate, since Wilson, too, took little heed of them, despite not wearing the guts.

He eventually did put the pancho back on, thankfully, because he was meticulous in refolding the hammock material. Wilson just couldn't handle the material sticking out of the hammock's tiny carrying bag. He was interrupted a half dozen times by zombies lurching towards him. When he had finally succeeded in returning the hammock to its pouch, there was a short wall of bodies surrounding him.

He had folded his OCD back up much like the hammock. His priority now was getting to the source of the sound as fast as possible, while drawing as little attention as possible. He drove himself into the increasingly tightly packed swarms of zombies, rubbing shoulders and everything else with the corpses. His fingers itched like poison ivy for some quality time with his moist towelettes.

He reached the center of the bridge over the Pilot Channel towards the end of the day. He was just in time to watch the fishing boat traveling upstream under the bridge. He called out to it, foolishly breaking cover smack in the middle of a swarm. His pancho did him little good, but it didn't matter. The onrush of zombies was too strong, and Wilson found himself falling over the side of the bridge.

The *Cajun Zombie Chronicles* continue in Book Three ...

The Kingdom Dead

Check it out on Amazon!

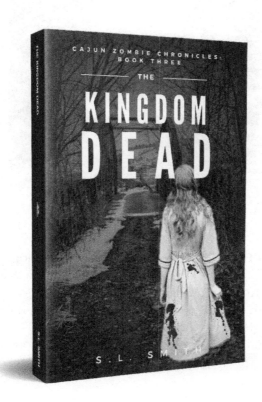

About the Author

Scott Smith is a Catholic author, attorney, and theologian. He and his wife Ashton are the parents of four wild-eyed children and live in their hometown of New Roads, Louisiana.

Smith is currently serving as the Chairman of the Men of the Immaculata, the Grand Knight of his local Knights of Columbus council, and a co-host of the Catholic Nerds Podcast. Smith has served as a minister and teacher far and wide: from Angola, Louisiana's maximum security prison, to the slums of Kibera, Kenya.

Smith is the author of the first pro-life horror novel, *The Seventh Word*. His other books include *Pray the Rosary with St. Pope John Paul II, The Catholic ManBook, Everything You Need to Know About Mary But Were Never Taught*, and *Blessed is He Who …* (Biographies of Blesseds).

Scott regularly contributes to his blog, "The Scott Smith Blog" at www.thescottsmithblog.com, WINNER of the 2018-2019 Fisher's Net Award for Best Catholic Blog:

Scott's other books can be found at his publisher's, Holy Water Books, website, holywaterbooks.com, as well as on Amazon.

His other books on theology and the Catholic faith include *The Catholic ManBook*, *Everything You Need to Know About Mary But Were Never Taught*, and *Blessed is He Who ...* (Biographies of Blesseds). More on these below ...

His fiction includes *The Seventh Word*, a pro-life horror novel, and the *Cajun Zombie Chronicles*, the Catholic version of the zombie apocalypse.

Pray, Hope, & Don't Worry:
Catholic Prayer Journal for Women

Scott also recently authored a series of prayer journals with his wife. *The Pray, Hope, & Don't Worry* Prayer Journal to Overcome Stress and Anxiety:

ALL
SAINTS
UNIVERSITY
EST. MMXVII

Scott has also produced courses on the Blessed Mother and Scripture for All Saints University.

Learn about the Blessed Mary from anywhere and learn to defend your mother! It includes over six hours of video plus a free copy of the next book … Enroll Now!

What You *Need* to Know About Mary
But Were Never Taught

Pray the Rosary
with St. John Paul II

St. John Paul II said "the Rosary is my favorite prayer." So what could possibly make praying the Rosary even better? Praying the Rosary with St. John Paul II!

This book includes a reflection from John Paul II for every mystery of the Rosary. You will find John Paul II's biblical reflections on the twenty mysteries of the Rosary that provide practical insights to help you not only understand the twenty mysteries but also live them.

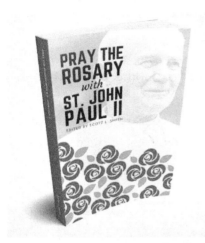

St. John Paul II said "The Rosary is my favorite prayer. A marvelous prayer! Marvelous in its simplicity and its depth. In the prayer we repeat many times the words that the Virgin Mary heard from the Archangel, and from her kinswoman Elizabeth."

St. John Paul II said "the Rosary is the storehouse of countless blessings." In this new book, he will help you dig even deeper into the treasures contained within the Rosary.

You will also learn St. John Paul II's spirituality of the Rosary: "To pray the Rosary is to hand over our burdens to the merciful hearts of Christ and His mother."

"The Rosary, though clearly Marian in character, is at heart a Christ-centered prayer. It has all the depth of the gospel message in its entirety. It is an echo of the prayer of Mary, her perennial Magnificat for the work of the redemptive Incarnation which began in her virginal womb."

Take the Rosary to a whole new level with St. John Paul the Great! St. John Paul II, *pray for us!*

Prayer Like a Warrior:
Spiritual Combat & War Room Prayer Guide

Don't get caught unarmed! Develop your Prayer Room Strategy and Battle Plan.

An invisible war rages around you. Something or someone is attacking you, unseen, unheard, yet felt throughout every aspect of your life. An army of demons under the banner of Satan has a singular focus: your destruction and that of everyone you know and love.

You need to protect your soul, your heart, your mind, your marriage, your children, your relationships, your resolve, your dreams, and your destiny.

Do you want to be a Prayer Warrior, but don't know where to start? The Devil's battle plan depends on catching you unarmed and unaware. If you're tired of being pushed around and wrecked by sin and distraction, this book is for you.

Do you feel uncomfortable speaking to God? Do you struggle with distractions in the presence of Almighty God? Praying to God may feel foreign, tedious, or like a ritual, and is He really listening? What if He never hears, never responds? This book will show you that God always listens and always answers.

In this book, you will learn how to prayer effectively no matter where you are mentally, what your needs are, or how you are feeling:

- Prayers when angry or your heart is troubled
- Prayers for fear, stress, and hopelessness
- Prayers to overcome pride, unforgiveness, and bitterness
- Prayers for rescue and shelter

Or are you looking to upgrade your prayer life? This book is for you, too. You already know that a prayer war room is a powerful weapon in spiritual warfare. Prepare for God to pour out blessings on your life.

113

Author, theologian, and attorney Scott L. Smith, Jr. has tested the prayers and wisdom of this book as a missionary in Africa, a minister in maximum security prisons, in the courtroom, and, most challenging of all, as a husband and father of four.

Our broken world and broken souls need the prayers and direction found in this book. Don't waste time fumbling through your prayer life. Pray more strategically when you have a War Room Battle Plan. Jesus showed His disciples how to pray and He wants to show you how to pray, too.

Catholic Nerds Podcast

As you might have noticed, Scott is obviously well-credentialed as a nerd. Check out Scott's podcast: the Catholic Nerds Podcast on iTunes, Podbean, Google Play, and wherever good podcasts are found!

What You Need to Know About Mary But Were Never Taught

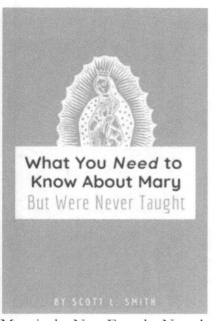

Give a robust defense of the Blessed Mother using Scripture. Now, more than ever, every Catholic needs to learn how to defend their mother, the Blessed Mother. Because now, more than ever, the family is under attack and needs its Mother.

Discover the love story, hidden within the whole of Scripture, of the Father for his daughter, the Holy Spirit for his spouse, and the Son for his MOTHER.

This collection of essays and the All Saints University course made to accompany it will demonstrate through Scripture how the Immaculate Conception of Mary was prophesied in Genesis.

It will also show how the Virgin Mary is the New Eve, the New Ark, and the New Queen of Israel.

The Catholic ManBook

Do you want to reach Catholic Man LEVEL: EXPERT? *The Catholic ManBook* is your handbook to achieving Sainthood, manly Sainthood. Find the following resources inside, plus many others:

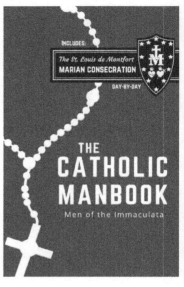

- Top Catholic Apps, Websites, and Blogs
- Everything you need to pray the Rosary
- The Most Effective Daily Prayers & Novenas, including the Emergency Novena
- Going to Confession and Eucharistic Adoration like a boss!
- Mastering the Catholic Liturgical Calendar

The Catholic ManBook contains the collective wisdom of The Men of the Immaculata, of saints, priests and laymen, fathers and sons, single and married. Holiness is at your fingertips. Get your copy today.

This edition also includes a revised and updated St. Louis de Montfort Marian consecration. Follow the prayers in a day-by-day format.

The Seventh Word
The FIRST Pro-Life Horror Novel!

Pro-Life hero, Abby Johnson, called it "legit scary ... I don't like reading this as night! ... It was good, it was so good ... it was terrifying, but good."

The First Word came with Cain, who killed the first child of man. The Third Word was Pharaoh's instruction to the midwives. The Fifth Word was carried from Herod to Bethlehem. One of the Lost Words dwelt among the Aztecs and hungered after their children.

Evil hides behind starched white masks. The ancient Aztec demon now conducts his affairs in the sterile environment of corporate medical facilities. An insatiable hunger draws the demon to a sleepy Louisiana hamlet.

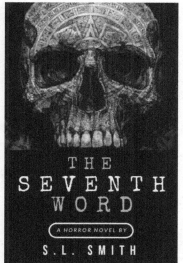

There, it contracts the services of a young attorney, Jim David, whose unborn child is the ultimate object of the demon's designs. Monsignor, a mysterious priest of unknown age and origin, labors unseen to save the soul of a small town hidden deep within Louisiana's plantation country, nearly forgotten in a bend of the Mississippi River.

You'll be gripped from start to heart-stopping finish in this page-turning thriller.

With roots in Bram Stoker's Dracula, this horror novel reads like Stephen King's classic stories of towns being slowly devoured by an unseen evil and the people who unite against it.

The book is set in southern Louisiana, an area the author brings to life with compelling detail based on his local knowledge.

Blessed is He Who ...
Models of Catholic Manhood

You are the average of the five people you spend the most time with, so spend more time with the Saints! Here are several men that you need to get to know whatever your age or station in life. These short biographies will give you an insight into how to live better, however you're living.

From Kings to computer nerds, old married couples to single teenagers, these men gave us extraordinary examples of holiness:

- Pier Giorgio Frassati & Carlo Acutis – Here are two ex-traordinary **young men**, an athlete and a computer nerd, living on either side of the 20th Century

- Two men of royal stock, Francesco II and Archduke Eu-gen, lived lives of holiness despite all the world conspir-ing against them.

- There's also the **simple husband and father**, Blessed Luigi. Though he wasn't a king, he can help all of us treat the women in our lives as queens.

Blessed Is He Who ... Models of Catholic Manhood explores the lives of six men who found their greatness in Christ and His Bride, the Church. In six succinct chapters, the authors, noted historian Brian J. Costello and theologian and attorney Scott L. Smith, share with you the uncommon lives of exceptional men who will one day be numbered among the Saints of Heaven, men who can bring all of us closer to sainthood.

THANKS FOR READ-
ING!
TOTUS TUUS

Made in the USA
Monee, IL
08 October 2022